zuckerbook

Jerry Zucker Middle School of Science
The Zuckerbook Project
2020 - 2021

Faculty Advisor
Mr. Erik J. Hilden

Copy Editing
Erik J. Hilden editor-in-chief
I'ris Gudrunardottir copy editor lead
Javier Green copy editor
Learric Green copy editor
Alex Ramos Ramos copy editor
Kaitlyn Williams copy editor

Art Department
Angela Gonzalez Gomez creative director
Jameson Perkins production artist & illistrator
Micah Edwards production artist & illustrator
Ulises Oliva Tellez production artist & illustrator

Social Media
Abigail Westbury social media lead
Brooke Cumbee social media
Yudi Cano Garcia social media
Victoria Flores social media

Marketing
Tori Odom marketing lead
Cole Palzer fundraising
Tyniece Graham fundraising

Cover Art **Ayleen Galvan**

Published by **The Zuckerbook Project,** ©2021, North Charleston, SC.

https://zuckerbook.square.site/
https://www.gofundme.com/f/funding-the-zuckerbook-project

© 2021 by **The Zuckerbook Project** in concert with:

The Students of Jerry Zucker Middle School of Science
6401 Dorchester Road Room 159
North Charleston, South Carolina 29418
Principal: Jacob Perlmutter
Assistant Principal: Andrea Gadsden
Assistant Principal: Shorace Guider

ISBN: 978-0-578-92551-6

Printed in the United States of America.

Dedication

This work is dedicated to the students
who created each piece that is contained
within these pages.
Their words, their art, their spirits,
and their energies bring this work to life.
May their voices always be heard.

Community Involvement

Endeavors such as these are evidence of the great things that can
happen when a community pulls together in the face of adversity and
produces a testament to the voices of their children. Without the support
of our community, this would not have been possible, and without further
support, future endeavors may not come to pass. We have had a lot of
support this year, but we can always use more, as is true of any non-
profit activity. If you are interested in donating to The Zuckerbook Project
or are interested in volunteering to help in any way, please feel free to get
in touch. I can be reached at **erik_hilden@charleston.k12.sc.us** or at
the following address:

The Zuckerbook Project c/o
Jerry Zucker Middle School of Science
6401 Dorchester Rd. Room 159
North Charleston, SC 29418
843-767-8383 ext. 25614
or 503-778-0393. We look forward to hearing from you.

Acknowledgements

In a year like no other, it can be difficult to know what to acknowledge. Does one point to the challenges we faced and our successes and failures despite said challenge? It feels trivial. This school year has, without question, been a year unlike any other in our lifetimes. Not to bemoan the apparent stresses involved, the change in dynamic changed the way business gets done. Students started the year online, even if some of them were in the building. How would we do this? It was a mystery.

And yet we did. Classes went from remote to in person. Never having taught this class online before, we were starting from scratch, with limited success, resulting in one Zuckerbook for this school year instead of our usual two volumes. All school-related fundraising ceased, even our regular quarter-long run of the school vending machine. Without those funds, we were in danger of not releasing anything this year. The generosity of our donors, both near and far, saved us and saved this publication.

Hopefully, next year things will return to something closer to normal. With gratitude, we dedicate this volume of Zuckerbook to those who generously supported us with donations and funneled artwork and original writing. Without them, we would have nothing to offer, and their support of the arts, this project, and the students at Jerry Zucker Middle School of Science is truly blessed.

I do hope we have not forgotten anyone. In the chaos of this school year, that is possible, so if that happened, please accept my most humble apologies.

Jacob Perlmutter is the reason that Zuckerbook exists. Without Jake, I would not even be here. He took me, a fledgling teacher, under his wing after convincing me to move across the country to join his faculty, leaving Portland, Oregon and everything I had ever known in the process. He navigated the ship that is Zucker Middle School across choppy seas and out of the near ruins of a previous administrator and turned it into what it is today - a place where the teachers want to teach and the students want to learn. Without his enthusiasm, there would likely not have been a guitar club, and there would not have been a Zuckerbook. His leaving these shores for the unchartered territory of another school, a school in need of his touch, his grace, his balance, and his talent for bringing people together, is among the greatest losses I can imagine. This volume of Zuckerbook is dedicated to him.

The entire faculty, administration, and staff of Zucker Middle School, our community and family, cohort and cadre, deserves a thank you for continuing to support our existence in these trying times. Thank you for your support.

Erin Presto made a selfless donation of funds to help us in production and brought us both artwork and writing from her students. I cannot express my appreciation for her support. Saying thank you is not enough.

Stephanie Platt, our Spanish teacher, donated to keep our dream of publishing student writing and art alive. Thank you, Ms. Daniels.

Carie Tyndall contributed selflessly toward the production of this volume with moral support and funds. Her support has been ongoing and is always greatly appreciated.

Dr. Clark G. Hilden, who has continued to donate to our cause, deserves special mention, for donating large amounts of money and inspiration, support for our students, and mentoring as we go forward in the unchartered waters of small batch publishing. Take a look at his textbook, *Uniquely Oregon*, if you want an interesting read about a fascinating state created by a dedicated teacher of geography. It is fun to read regardless of your interests, and available at Amazon.com.

Rhea Farmer has supported us for a few volumes now and is among my oldest friends. Our friendship goes back fifty years, and her support means the world to me. Thank you, Rhea.

Eileen and Ken Babbs are very special to me. Ken Babbs, who I met at my senior prom, is a famous writer and counterculture figure immortalized in such works as The Electric Kool-Aid Acid Test and was a long-time friend and collaborator with Ken Kesey, author of One Flew Over the Cuckoo's Nest and Sometimes a Great Notion. His partner, Eileen Babbs, was my high school English teacher and Journalism teacher and has remained in my life as a mentor and friend. Their support is massive, and I couldn't be more pleased to have them in our corner. Thank you, guys. Thank you.

James Brooks retired at the end of the 2016-2017 school year and is sorely missed. His support for The Zuckerbook Project was unwaivering, and his assistance in assembling the best crew possible for each year was invaluable in setting the standards for this class and this publication. We remain in his debt and envious of his retirement.

Kellie King is an old and dear friend from the days when we were in the public school trenches in Pendleton, Oregon. Her support is fantastic and much appreciated. Thank you again and again, Kellie.

Gina Harris and **Mike Harris** have repeatedly taken it upon themselves to promote The Zuckerbook Project by traveling the world and snapping prictures of Zuckerbook in the hands of children. A trip to Guatemala had them leave a copy in the hands of a young boy whose father began to teach him English by reading Zuckerbook. Unbelievable. Thank you.

Bridget Means of BridgetMeansDesign.com started helping us when Zuckerbook was produced on a laser printed and assembled with a stapler. She brought us out of the "obviously school made" realm into the world of the professional look, working with us to create a brand identity and dedicating her design studio to each issue of Zuckerbook twice per year at an unheard of discount. There is no way to thank her for her work other than to say that without her, we wouldn't be here. This year, she donated her time and expertise free of charge.

Jason Waite donated much needed funds to support our project this year and did so as a complete surprise to us. Thank you, good sir. We are grateful for your generosity.

Shosana Driver is an old and dear friend from my heady days at The Evergreen State College. Always a generous and profound soul, her friendship over the years is a treasure to me and her support of what we are doing at The Zuckerbook Project is huge. Thank you, Shosh, from the bottom of our hearts.

Sarah Callahan remains, and always shall remain, a spirit guide on our journey. Zuckerbook started, in part, because of her, and though she is taking time off from teaching to raise a family, she remains within the pages of this book. Bless her and the work that she does. She is a jewel in the crown of education and teaching.

The Mission of The Zuckerbook Project is to produce the very highest quality student publication of literary works mixed with visual art, while remaining faithful to the Zucker Middle School student experience so that our voices may be heard. Let them always be heard.

Open it and read...

-- Mr. Erik J. Hilden, June 3rd, 2021

Zuckerbook in Cambodia.   *photos by Gina Harris*

zuckerbook

Contents

Prologue

Since a prologue is, by nature, a way of introducing the book and letting the reader shake its hand, we thought we would write yet another one. There are always plenty of surprises.

How to introduce each chapter is not so simple a task. That has never stopped us before. There is no reason for it to stop us now.

O! The Fury! explores the depths of teen angst from our corner of the universe. Why not get mad and spray our anger all over a page? Indeed.

All The Sappy Feels connects the reader to the teenage experience of rolller-coaster emotions and sentimental exporations into the caverns of the pubescent heart.

Invisible Enemies offers a long, cold stare into the face of the biggest challenge any of us have had to handle to date. The teenage perspective is potent.

Faceless explores invisibility, pure and simple. What is it like to be unseen?

On Love And Hate is another dance on the stage of the teenage heart, focusing this time on the various ways we feel when true romance blossoms or goes sour.

Sorry Not Sorry is what you get when you tell kids to tell you what they think and to not care about what anyone else thinks about what they think. Yes indeed, they most certainly are NOT sorry.

Five By Seven By Five hammers out haiku int the age of online learning and other strangeness. Why not make it five by seven by five?

Freestyle is exactly that - a collection of poems springing from the freedom of writing whatever you want, about whatever you want, in any way you choose. Isn't freedom grand?

Happy Endings? presents the fairy tale, filtered through the mind of the Honors English I class. Happy endings, a indeed.

A Sonnet In Your Bonnet is another collection of student sonnets. heavily inspired by Shakespeare.

By The Numbers is a collection of poems that draws inpiration from numbers, the classroom, the students, their friends, and everything else, and brings our latest volume to a close. We finish by looking to the past and the future.

Enjoy.

EJH

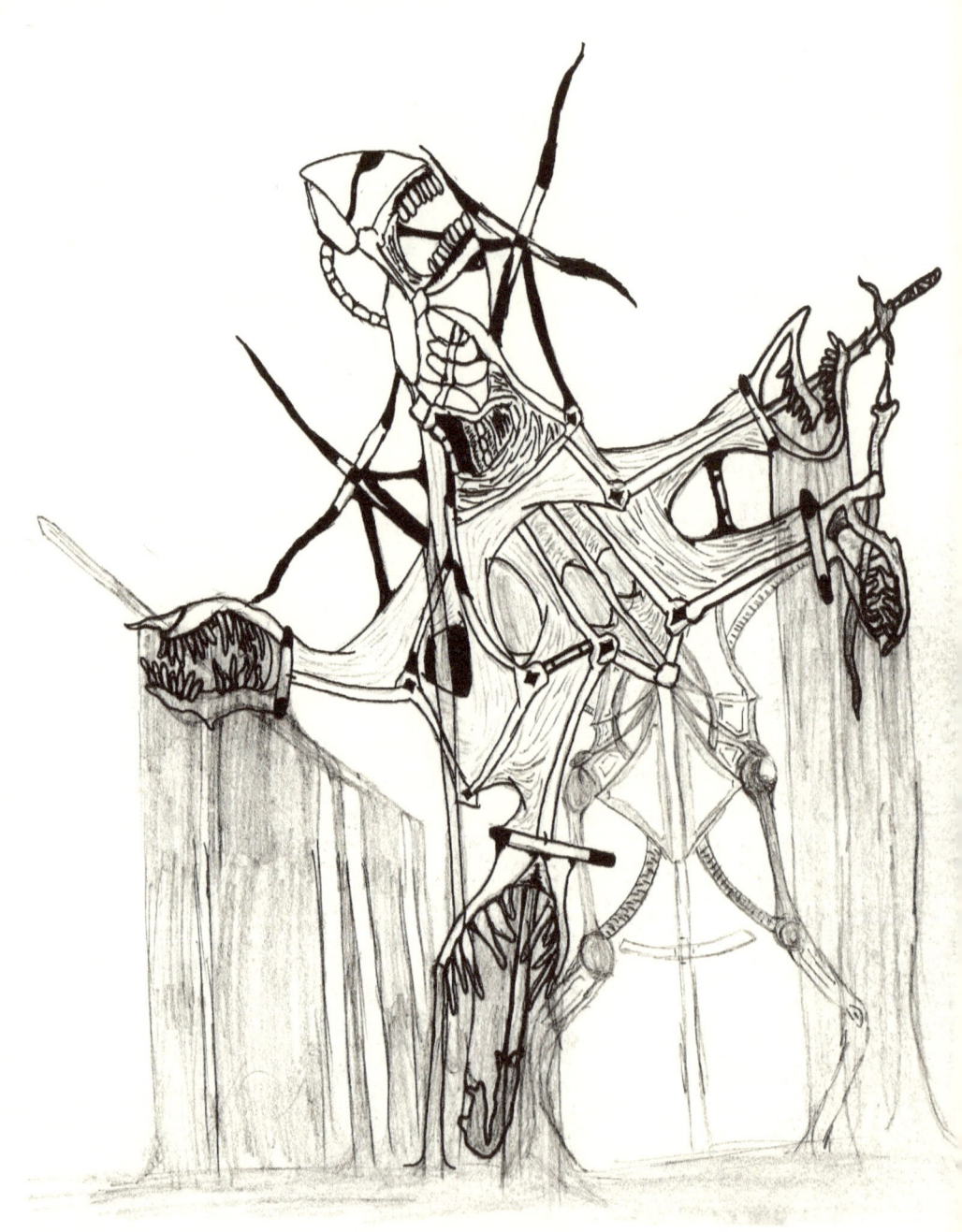

Jameson Perkins

1 O! The Fury!

Tick Me Off

Ulises Oliva Tellez

These flies really tick me off.
They bite me all-day.
I wish they were all dead.
Because they turn me all red.

But all you can do is hate on them.
You can't make them go extinct.
But you can make them stay away from you,
And the lifesaver is bug spray.

Spray on some bug spray on you.
You wouldn't regret it.
Now you don't have to worry.
Just don't be such an angry bird.

No One Is The Same

Traquam Jones

They say I am different.
I say everyone is different.
I am different and so are you.
Nobody is the same.

They say I am not perfect.
I say no one is perfect.
I am not perfect but I am good.
Everyone is not perfect all the time.

They say I have autism.
I say I am not the only one.
I am glad to have autism.
It can be hard, but I'm happy about it.

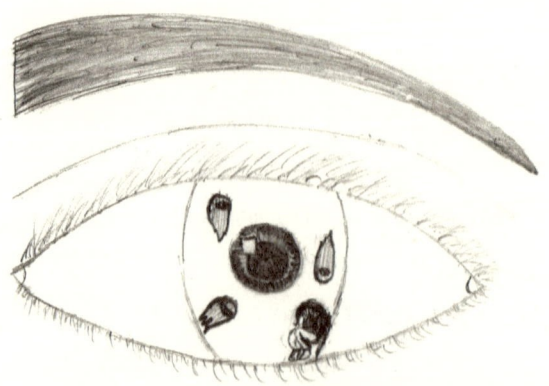

Angela Gomez

Human

Hailee Gudrunardottir

Everywhere I look, there has to be
Some sort of discrimination.
Humans from ages 6 to everyone.
They laugh, mock, steal, and belittle them.
Just humans being human.

Some people have no houses.
There are people with no food and nourishment.
But, some people think they have the high ground,
And they think of us as the lesser beings.

We're humans, you and I.
Nothing more, nothing less.
We are the same.
Humans, that's all.

My Body

Yudi Cano

I don't like looking in the mirror scared that
My image won't' help my day.
Scared of feeling like I am not enough,
Scared to see other imperfection.
But people say my skin looks so beautiful in the sun.

Yet I don't feel like that.
Your lips are so beautiful,
Pinkish color yet I put more lipstick.
I walk into class with my
Imperfection and a girl stops me
And says wow your Acne is getting
worse do you even take care of it?

I know if I love my self a little more
I won't care as much,
But am I wrong to not love myself
When the world tells me
I am not good enough each day?

And at that moment the world seems to stop
She felt okay everything seem okay
The world didn't seem against her
We are okay, she said.

Madness

Brooke Cumbee

Anger makes you boil.
It will slowly poison you and others,
Corrupting everyone around you.
The anger will reach new levels.

It will mess up everything,
If you have worked for it,
Or if someone else has worked for it,
If it takes over you will always be corrupted.

You will drown if you get caught in it.
The poison will ruin your life.
The poison will take over.
The poison is anger.

Ulises Oliva Tellez

Repeat Nothing

Micah Edwards

Repeating the day again, as annoying as it can be.
Not knowing how much of what the day will bring,
Waking up to the smacking of
cereal, chomping, mussy, disgusting.

I try to ignore it without fussing.
Still tired, I try to do something,
But in boredom I find nothing.
The lack of things I find makes me weep.

And even though I just woke up, I want to
Go back to sleep, though I try my best.
All the background noise gives me stress.
Another day, another road they say,

But all the day feels like a delay.

Don't Mess With My Stuff.

Tyniece Graham

I told my siblings to not mess with my video games.
They wouldn't listen, so I broke their toys.
They called me that he was mad,
And cruel behind my back.
But I didn't mind, they can call me what they want.

Don't eat my stuff in the fridge.
That is not a very nice thing to do,
But my siblings don't think so.
Every day I come back from school, my food is gone.
I asked them who did it but no one will confess.

So I took all of their candy
From when they went trick or treating.
They cried and asked who stole all of their candy.
They asked everyone
Who messed with their candy.
Then they came to me.
I replied with don't mess with my stuff.

Judgment

Hailee Gudrunardottir

Why do you look at people and say,
"Look at the way she dresses..."
And think it's okay?
You're leaving emotional messes.

You go around and judge others,
But look at yourself in the mirror and
BAM! You're not as perfect as another.
But, you go out of your way to bother others.

Just give up, we don't like people like you.
It's not right or polite to be this absurd.
In the future, I'm not sure if you knew
There'll be a time where you get what you deserve.

There is a thing called 'Karma.'
She goes to everyone from woman to man.
One thing you need to know
Is that with your problems,
She doesn't give a damn.

Trash

Ulises Oliva Tellez

These games are trash
That's All I can say
I throw my controller
I punch the walls

I say I won't play anymore
I play the next day
The same thing happens
Don't rage they all say

We all get mad
We all throw fits
All you gotta do is be calm
Just don't get mad

Angela Gomez

Mind Control

Jameson O. Perkins

Control is all the world knows of,
All the politicians think. And how they act,
They tell us they'll make a better future,
While in reality they just do it for the rich.

School needs a bit of order,
But people just feed the schools to it,
We let it grow bigger and bigger,
Then it comes with a cost: Humanity,

People are told to do this and do that,
They think that control is good
When enforced, and at first yes it is,
But they've taken it way too far.

People are told they're doing criminal behavior
Just for making an airplane without even throwing it.
They exploit the education system
By making it mind-numbing,
And yet they think it will help their kids.

Get Upset

Angela Gonzalez

I get mad and you get upset.
Is it my fault that I have to carry this anger?
Because of you, because you couldn't control
Yourself and had to be so annoying.

It irritated me knowing that if you get mad,
I get mad, and I hate feeling like that.
Can't I just get a break?
But no, because then,
There you go again
And madness come up in my head.

Emma Daley

I Had To Write A Poem

Elliott Avila

So this day I had to write a poem.
The type of poem I don't know what to write.
The poem of me being an idiot.
I am writing a poem that doesn't have anything
But just me not knowing what to write.

That type of poem that makes you feel
Like you have a stinky brain.
But if I did know what to write in a poem,
I would have a nice looking poem.

While I'm writing this poem of nothing,
I am thinking in my little brain.
What to write in this poem? I can
Only think of a poem with
Nothing in my head.

No rhyming or anything.
I heard a ringtone on a
Hidden overpriced calculator, meaning
I only have a few minutes
To write, to finish the
Poem of nothing.

This is the type of poem of nothing
That has nothing. And it should.

The 'Karen' Outbreak

Hailee Gudrunardottir

Around the internet
There are these 'Karens' around.
They yell, scream, and call the cops.
They are unstoppable.

They freak out over little things,
Such as store prices and someone's hair.
They call for the store manager,
And they don't even care.

They refuse to wear their masks
Because they 'violate their rights.'
They yell at you for not believing in
Jesus Christ.

If you see a wild Karen around,
Look out!
Because, I swear, one day,
I will dropkick one,
And I won't feel any remorse.

Hate You

Brooke Cumbee

When I said I hated you,
I meant I hated you.
It was the feeling you gave me
When you walked into the room.

The things you did to annoy me.
The things you said to get me upset.
I let you win this time.
Next time I will get you.

The things you say.
The things you do.
The things you make me do.
The things you make me say.

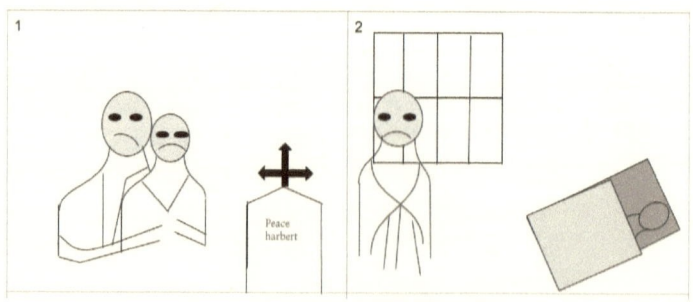

Angela Gomez

The New Virus

Jameson O. Perkins

There is a new virus,
That kills adults and their kids.
One was people think to believe
That the worse will come.
That is the virus of stupidity.

None of them care at all.
They have almost no brain cells.
Which would make sense for the most part.
They act like they're smart,
But their brains have no gears.

I hear excuse after excuse.
"It gives kids autism."
"It's the devils' work."
They all sound like idiots.

To be honest,
I'm surprised to know
People who are like that.
Their parents brainwashed them into believing.
I hate this virus and we need a cure for it.

Lemons

Kaitlyn Williams.

When life gives you lemons,
Make lemonade.
In this case, I'm life.
But I have no lemons.
Guess I'll have to stay thirsty.

Every time I get a chance
To make some lemonade,
I always run out of something,
Be it a clean pitcher or clean water.

The lemons have gone bad
Or aren't ripe yet.
The sugar turns out to be flour
Or I've run out.

So when life gives you lemons
You might as well shove them
Where the sun don't shine
Cause you sure aren't gonna
See any lemonade.

Make Me Wanna Shout

Ulises Oliva Tellez

A lot of people annoy me.
They get me all mad.
They make me wanna shout.
All I wanna do is punch them.

They say this.
They say that.
They say all of this to me.
This is all bullcrap.

I get mad easily.
I don't know how to act.
I should stop getting mad.
I shold make a pact

With the morons who annoy me
And the people who shout.
Punching solves nothing.
Just move on.

Ulises Oliva Tellez

Commercials

Learric Green

They appear everytime you try to watch tv.
It's always this terrible short that you can't avoid.
Always opening with people who have on
fake smiles and fake reactions,

Never ending, always showing off
products that appeal to no one.
And there is always many of these every 10 minutes.
It's just a never ending show of

"Do you struggle from this?"
"Don't you think you need this in your life?"
Always 30 seconds long.
The acting makes them look like robots.

And sometimes you don't even get a different ad.
The same ad can come up
Multiple times in 15 minutes,
And they always have this number that goes

Call now at 165964032187-Fast

Mindless Typing Now

Tatiana Diaz Mayen

Mindless typing now.
To what end? Another prem?
How is this English?

What's justice these days?
Does it have any meaning?
Why in my own house?

I was just going out.
I just wanted to go out.
Why, me out of all.

Out of all places.
Why here, It is time to hide.
What are they doing?

How to tell someone
They're always picking on me.
Will it get worse, though?

Caden Winters

Humiliation

Jack Garcia Linarte

Humiliation.
Going through it is scary
But I got back up.

I can't trust myself.
It was super dumb of me.
I thought good things now.

I believe in BLM.
Nobody is different.
I believe in that.

Bullying is wrong,
But it happens every day.
I will not stand for it.

I have never known why
People think it's cool to judge.
It is super dumb.

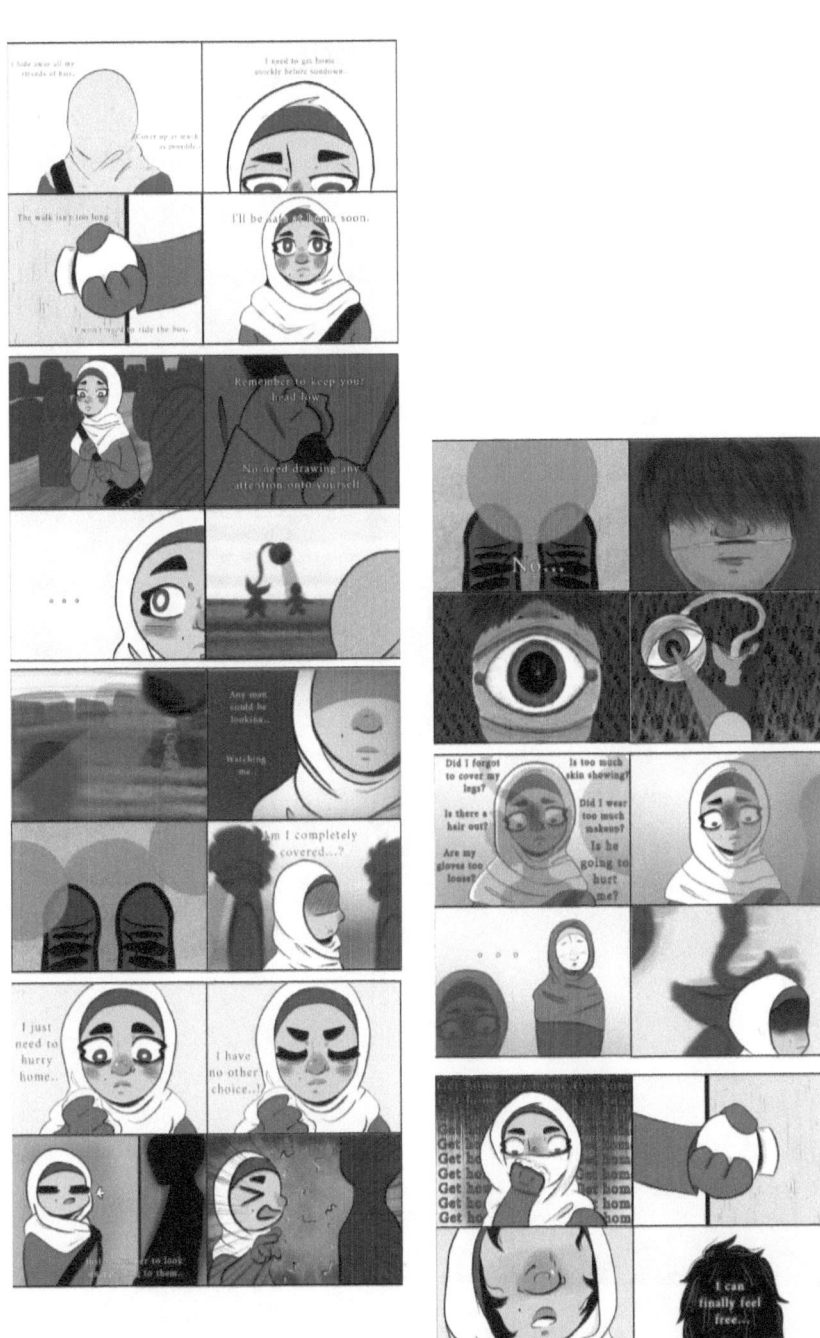

Teandra Johnson

Angela Gomez

2 All The Sappy Feels

Sunset

Ruby Cedillo

Sunset after a day goes by.
Moonrise when the light escapes.
Stars shine as they always have
Whether or not there are clouds overhead.

Sunset after a life poorly lived.
Moonrise in honor of bleak escape.
Stars break free of the soul that is lost,
And find another means for existence.

Sunset after the dawn of time.
Moonrise brighter than all if the fire.
Stars walk red paths into boxes of stupidity,
Eyes glued down, never blinking.

I Miss Those Times

Brook Cumbee

I miss those old times.
I miss those times.
I miss your tight hugs and your warm body.
And those silly faces you would make,
That feeling when you walk into the room.

I've counted the days and nights.
I have watched the sunset waiting for you
To come back to town.
I am waiting for you in this lonely place.

Everything has turned to gray.
When I can't look to my side to you,
I am stuck here without anyone.
If only I could bring back the good old days.

I wonder how he is doing.
I wonder if he is reminiscing about us.
Thinking about the place we would hang out
When we would play around and have fun.

Looking Back

Micah Edwards

Looking back on past we see all the things we enjoy.
Whether that be us hanging out with friends
Or going to the places we love,
2021 has had many setbacks.

If only our nostalgia was as small bug.
But we can't just forget the things we miss and love,
Like having fun during the Summer.
Don't let the days bring you down to a bummer.

Though we look back at the Past
And Remember all the time was had a blast,
Those Feelings will come back soon.
Just you wait and see.

Ulises Oliva Tellez

Walk Through A Garden

Vicky Flores

I walk through a garden with bright red roses.
Looking around in my dark beautiful gown,
Strolling through at night,
My hair flowing in front of my face,

Wishing I could stay here forever.
Not wanting to forget the peace.
Hearing the calming sounds of the waterfall,
In the fog, there is a man.

A man with a light brown coat on,
Gorgeous eyes and dark hair.
I walk towards him, reaching out for his hand.
I suddenly wake up knowing it wasn't real.

Ulises Oliva Tellez

When We Were Young

Angela Gonzalez Gomez

When we were young we wouldn't
Have to worry about anything as we do now.
During the sunny days at the park running around,
And if we get hurt our mother would be there for us.

Know that we have grown.
We don't get help because we can do it ourselves,
But back then, a person would help us
And tell us it would be okay.

Back then, I had time more than I could
Ever had and I would spend time with.
My friends and going to the swings and see who
Goes the highest but know I barely have time.

When We Did Not Have To Wear A Mask

Tyniece Graham

There were times where we
Did not have to wear a mask.
We would go outside and play
With our friends, and family.

Go to parties and hangout
With our family and friends.
Be able to touch, and hug
Our family and friends.

But now that has changed
Because of this dreaded virus.
There were times where we
Did not have to wear a mask.

We would all go to school,
Come back and do whatever
We had to do.
Go to your community

Pool and playground.
In stores we didn't have
to be six feet apart.
There were times where we

Did not have to wear a mask.
And even though we never
Had to wear a mask before 2020,
you now have to remember

To wear a mask.
So wear your mask.

Stagger Stagger, Roll Roll

Abigail Westbury

The beach, calm, beautiful, blue.
Everyone loves the beach, the waves, the breeze,
Sandy toes and sunkissed nose.

Parents and children,
Boats, surfing, swimming,
Doing what they love.

Volleyball, tennis, running and jumping,
Hopping,
Skipping,
Running,

Stagger Stagger, Roll Roll
Stumble Fall Thump.

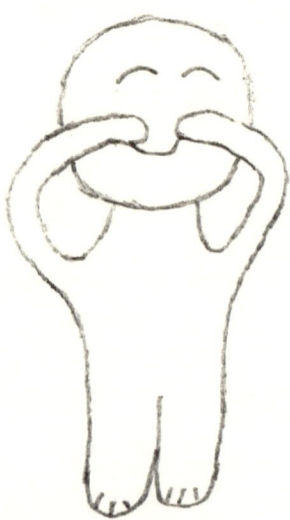

Ulises Oliva Tellez

The World

Learric Green

When I was still in elementary school,
The world looked so clean.
It looked like it had no type of evil
Walking on the same giant rock.

The trees and rocks shined under the sunlight
The clouds glowed like they contained
A little bit of light inside them
The sky a bright and young blue color,

But now the sky is filled with smoke.
Trees cut down, removing some animal's homes,
Litter everywhere on the ground,
Even next to a trash can.

Fires burning down everything,
A new virus making people lock away
The outside world.
Faces have to be hidden, smiles erased.

Mama

Kaitlyn Williams

I know you weren't expecting this.
But you taught me everything.
You are always there for me,
And no one else will be.

Mama, you know I love you.
I know I might not act like it,
And I'm sorry for that.
Nobody will ever love you as much as I do.

In my life, there were so many times
When I was afraid.
Nobody else can be
What you've been to me.
No one else can or will do
What you have done for me.

"It's not easy being a mother.
If it were easy, fathers would do it."
And Mama, I just want you
To know that loving you
And being your child
Is good enough for me.

I love you.

Watching Them Is Happiness

Maily Martinez

Watching them is my happiness.
They teach me new things every day.
They say, "love yourself."
I say,"i'm starting to love myself."

Now I see how beautiful I am.
Now I know "life goes on,"
No matter what my "life goes on" to.
Now I'm someone who loves herself so much.

I wake up and think about
how much I have changed.
I see myself as a different person now.
I realize what a good person I am.
But I'm still learning how to myself.

I still want to change things in me,
But I won't stop till
I love myself all the way.

Handles Of The Basket

Vicky Flores

Laughing and giggling with my cousin,
The sun shining in our faces,
Taking silly pictures on our phones.
In the car, on the way to a park.

As we arrive, she grabs the handles of the basket.
We sit down on a red-patched picnic blanket
Waiting for friends to show up.
She starts setting up the picnic area and I help along.

Friends finally show up.
We all huddle together giving each other hugs,
Eating amazing foods they brought,
And watching the pink sky as the sun rises down.

Back Then

Hailee Gudrunardottir

Remember back then?
We'd run around screaming, laughing,
Just doing stupid stuff
Until we were tired?

Remember back then?
We'd play, take naps
And eat sweets until
We couldn't eat anymore?

Remember back then?
When we got out of middle school
And promised we'd never forget our time together?
Yeah, I remember that.

Places

Learric Green

At the park playing on the playground
In the summer heat, the swings were the
Best part of the whole thing. Going down
The slides that felt like smooth and cozy ride,

The wood chips that gave you a sharp
Pain when you fell in them the only
Problem was bettime. Driving to the beach
Though the waves of heat, going out and

Enjoying the sand and water nature provided,
Playing with a beach ball and digging in the sand,
Running down the waves of the sand,
The next stop was a amusement park

Ulises Oliva Tellez

Where they had all the ride to see some
That can make you vomit others that make
You feel like you are in a cradle. The heart
Stopping rides that dropped when nobody

Would expect it to, tickets were not cheap,
But neither was a good time outside.
The Aquarium filled with fish. It was like
Everything was there. Sharks that snap

At the glass, seals that flowed with the
Water, a school of fish that instantly
Got scared when you slightly tap the glass.
There were too many to name or even to count.

The blue covered you.

We're Bulletproof

Hailee Gudrunardottir

It was rough in the beginning.
We fought, argued, cried, and had a lot of hatred in us.
We worked through it because we're a team.
We stick together no matter what comes our way.

Throughout the years, we've had hate.
Throughout the years, we've had heartbreak.
But we didn't let that break us down.
We're stronger than them.

The sun is setting.
The moon is brightening the night sky.
No one will get in our way to belittle us
Because we're bulletproof.

Ulises Oliva Tellez

Like Fireflies

Ruby Cedillo

Yellow lights flickering on and off like fireflies.
People lining up to la vibora de la mar, mimicking a snake.
Kids asleep on chairs with spilled drinks
And candy wrappers.
The cow already jumped over the moon by now.

The fiesta lights charged at you every time you looked around.
Secrets in re-used gifting bags waiting to be opened.
Beer being handed out like it's
Candy, over and over.
Nothing is out of the ordinary.

This kind of ritual happens over small things,
No matter the circumstances.
When morning comes, you have headaches,
Body aches, and a bloated stomach.
Wash, rinse, repeat, the sequel begins

Life Is Like A Bird

Darrell Goss

The Christmas tree was as green as the grinch
And as tall as my basketball court.
The coffee was as brown as the gingerbread man
And as hot as fire.

The candy cane was as red as blood and
Was white as paper.
The eggnog was as white as milk
And small like a pencil.

Santa was as big as a car
And as pale as a ghost.
The elves were as short as chair and
Ears were sharp like a pencil.

The School was tall as a hotel
and as wide as 100 fences.
The lunch was rocks and garbage,
And sometimes cold.

The bathrooms were dirty
And sometimes stink.
The water was cold and
The water fountain was dirty.

Some of the teachers were good but
Some were extra.
The gym was sometimes clean
But not always.

Life is like a bird
We fly to where we want
We live as we want
But there is always a bad thing

Who wants us gone,
Keeps us up at night,
Falling to our dreams with dry tears,
Acting as if we are OK.

Makes us depressed, stressed.
Smiling is not part of me.
My mind is a bag that is full,
About to explode.

Life is full of sadness.
Sadness that feels like
It won't go away

Ulises Oliva Tellez

See You Soon

Hailee Gudrunardottir

It's summertime.
The school year has ended.
As the students leave,
The crisp, summer breeze blow past them.

As we walk through the green grass,
The children are outside playing.
The parents are baking and relaxing.
The cool, clear water squirts out from

The water guns as the dogs play in it.
Summer break gives us stories to tell.
Summer break brings us new friendships.
Summer break may tear us apart.

But I'll see you soon in the end

The Memories

Brooke Cumbee

When we played with sticks like there was no tomorrow,
When we would run down the dirt road,
When we would jump in the pond,
When we thought parkour was jumping off the patio ledge.

The memories of hanging out with your cousins.
The memories of actually playing outside for hours on end.
The memories of the times where we met up
And didn't just facetime.
The memories of the time before we had phones.

The times when we would talk.
The times when we would play games in the car.
The times when we would write school work on paper.
The times when we were fun.

Emma Daley

Natural Habitat

Learric Green

Our first summer break had started.
The bell rang and we ran as fast as lighting,
Escaping the prison that is called school.
It was like we had the whole world to ourselves.

Every kid was outside like it was their natural habitat.
The flowers bursted with color and the birds
Waved at us from up above, the rocks were
Mountains that nobody would dare try to climb.

The neighborhood seemed to have
Gained twice the population than before,
Dodging people on bikes and hoverboards like
There was no tomorrow. So many people were

Outside it made the ground rumble. Sword
Fighting with sticks under the trees, the grass
Growing and brushing against our ankles,
Throwing a football as high as we could.

Playing basketball and missing every shot,
Rolling down in the grass and down some hills,
Even staying inside was a pleasure to some.
Even at night it seemed half the neighborhood.

Was outside enjoying the days of summer
The sound of people outside made it seem
like your house had no walls. It was loud...the
Sound things hitting the ground was

Constant but that didn't make anyone upset.
Nobody was upset with the many weeks
They had off for summer break. There were
Thousands of things to do during those days off.

Traveling with family and getting new toys to use,
It seemed like the fun might never end.

Ulises Oliva Tellez

Set Sail!

Hailee Gudrunardottir

Well, now those days are over.
No more toys, games, or bubbles.
We've had fun running around
And finding 4 leaf clovers.

Just because we are going our own separate ways,
Doesn't mean we can't still be near each other.
Just know I'm here for you always,
And you're there for me.

So set sail for the new world.
Let's live life like it's ending.
Don't worry about me, I'll be fine.
Goodbye, I'll see you next time!

Iris Gudrunardottir

To The Past

Ulises Olivas Tellez

Let's go to the past.
I want to see everything again
All the days go fast.
We were all ten back then.

Wish I could time travel.
That's what we all want.
All we did was pick gravel.
All we did was chant.

We can't relive those days.
All we can do is remember.
We all had our own ways.
The ways that made everything better.

Friends

Hailee Gudrunardottir

One friend is kind and generous,
The other mean and selfish.
The third one is popular and courageous.
The last is shy and weak.

What makes these friends so special?
Why do you have them around?
Why do you think they're good friends?
They're not as good as they sound.

Yeah, sure. They're not perfect,
But they're there for me.
That's what good friends do,
And I'm sure they'll never leave.

Ulises Oliva Tellez

Turn Back Time

Ulises Olivas Tellez

Wish I could turn back time
To the good old days.
All the nostalgia I feel
It's all real.

I want to go back
To the real world.
Don't want to suffer anymore,
Just wanna go home.

I want to see what I used to be.
I wanna see the past again.
The life back then was great.
I have all these sappy feels.

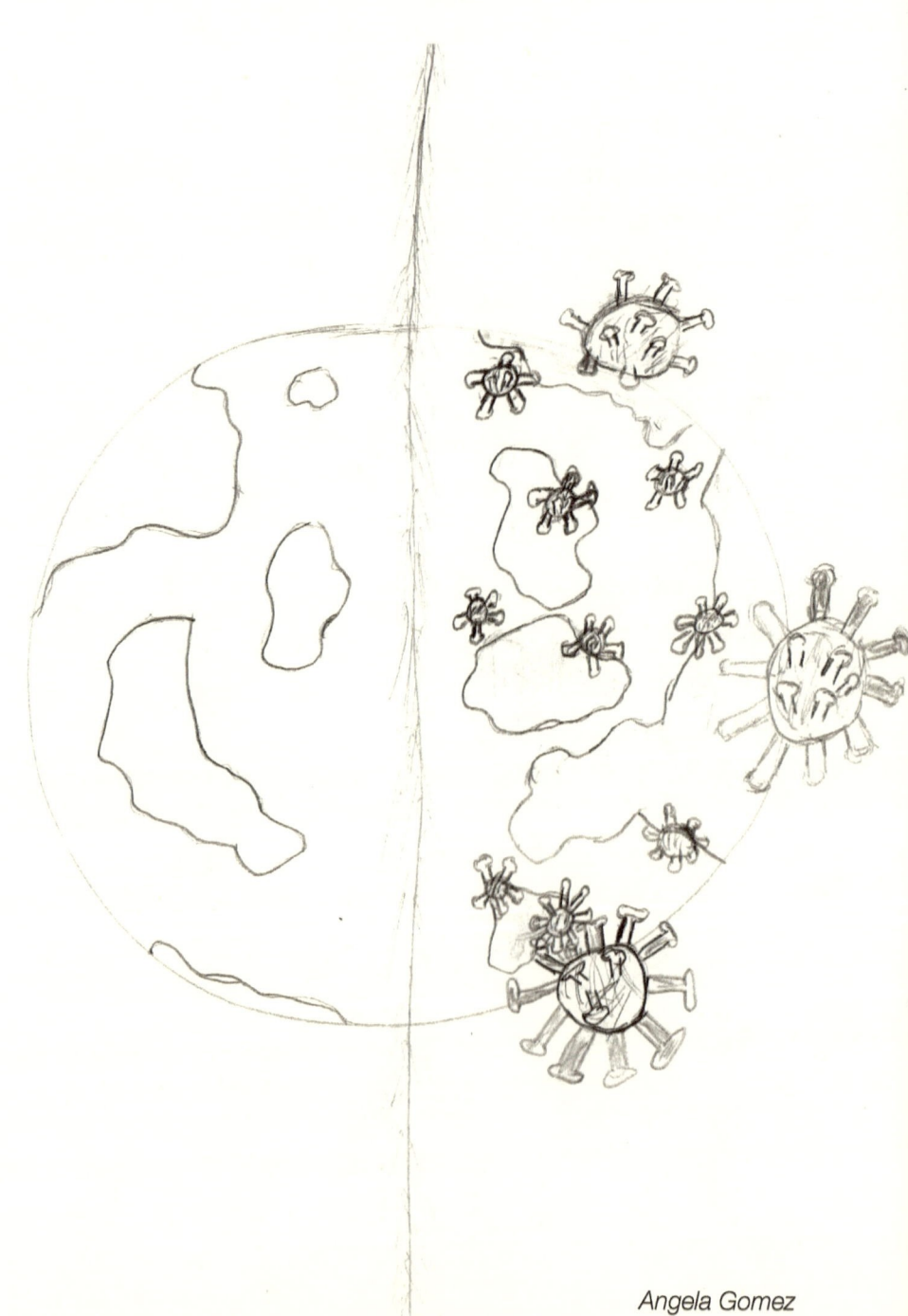

Angela Gomez

3 Invisible Enemies

Being Pushed

Mark Chavez

Being pushed,
Being challenged,
No help, just alone.
Any day, now, I can break.

Some people can already see it happening.
Only one actually cares.
Being on your limit and trying to push more.
But the pushing will just beat me down more.

The Sound Of Music

Mark Chavez

The sound of music.
The sound of chatter.
The night is supposed to be quiet.
Quiet it isn't.

All the racket at night
The neighbors are so quiet.
All the noise at night is waking me.
Not able to sleep.

They can get annoying.
They can be nice.
But can get on your nerve.
They can make the wrong choices.

Iris Gudrunardottir

They can get you into things that you can't get out of
Rarely serious work, mostly jokes.
Getting stuff done can be a challenge,
But they can be useful.

Being alone.
It can be fun for some.
Can suck for others.
Having only one on my side.

Something to cherish.
But know that they can leave.
Knowing that anyone can leave.
Just leave and leave you alone to suffer.

A Virus In Attack Mode

Chardnay Griffin

A nasty virus is her.
I hate it, just go away .
We can't do nothing any more.
I just want the virus to be gone.

People spreading the germ.
People making others angry.
Just go away already.
I really can't stand it.

Ghosts

Ahmyah Jackson

Are you a ghost or something?
You're there but you're not.
You said you'll never leave by my side
But you're never there.

Same thing with ghosts. They're there but they aren't.
It's in your imagination, but are you imaginary too?
It's possible to be someone's peace and disturbance
And you are that.

Grandfather Snails

Mia Mccoy

These people were getting sick like old grandfather snails.
People catching cases like a game of tag.
Not wearing their masks is a Karen fail.
Quarantine is like a chore.
Can't do anything until it is done.

Stuck in the house after
I finished my chores.
Finally done with torture, my work here
Is done.
There's still nothing to do
in this boring old home.
Being here is like a boring old
Museum,

'Til it done run its course.
A race against time and mortality,
But time is never going to end.
Where the only ones who win
Are the last ones standing,
And the other ones are going to be dead.

Oh, COVID!

Iliana Domenech

Oh, COVID, how unexpected you were.
COVID, COVID it has been a year now and you're still here.
And I have a question for you, when will you ever end?

Oh, COVID, You are like a shadow and yet you
Can hurt people. You followed everyone around, almost
Like you were everyone's shadow. You were a stranger
To the world. Oh, COVID, when will you ever end?

Oh, COVID, you took away my 5th-grade graduation.
People have suffered from you.
You have hurt many families around the world.
 Oh, COVID, when will you ever end?

Oh, COVID, because of you we must wear a mask,
Social distance and always put on hand sanitizer.
I cannot even hang out with my friends.

Oh, COVID, you hit my family hard
My aunt was seriously sick because of you.
You have made millions and millions of people lose their jobs.
Oh, COVID, when will you ever end?

But, COVID, one thing I will say is that you brought
my family together.
We got to spend time together. Time we did not have before.
You did that to a lot of families. A lot of people helped a lot
of people around the world too.
Oh, COVID, When will you ever end?

Oh, COVID, I am so thankful that you brought my family
closer together and other families too.
You have brought out kindness in people.
People are taking care of other people.
But Oh, COVID, when will you ever end?

Oh, COVID, I know that when you came into this world
people were mad at you.
Though I am happy you brought families closer than ever!
Oh, COVID, I only have one question for you
When will you ever end?

Locked Away

Hailee Gudrunardottir

March 15th, 2020, was the first day of quarantine
Everyone locked away in their homes
All the store's stocks are gone
People terrified of this virus

June 12th, 2020, virtual learning has ended. For now
All kids are bored inside their homes
Most places still closed for some time
People wearing masks for protection

August 21st, 2020, It's the start of a new school year for
kids and adults
Teachers teaching through a screen
Students stuck at home
And parents risking their lives to go outside
Everything

Ending And Beginning

Hailee Gudrunardottir

December 31, 2020
It's 11:59 pm
20 more seconds to midnight
The year has gone by fast
And people everywhere have died

We've accepted this new life as a new one
It'll be normal for all of us now
Here comes the countdown
10...9... 8...

To our new life, locked away
5...4...3...
2...1...
Chapter 2: 2021.

Iris Gudrunardottir

Invisible Enemies

Erol Blake

Covid-19 is like coal. No one wants it for Christmas.
The virus is affecting Christmas and stopping it
From happening.
Just like the Grinch who hated Christmas,
Covid is coal in an old dirty sock.

No one wants coal for Christmas.
Only bad kids get coal,
And the coal this year is
Covid and we all gettin' it.
Are we all bad kids this year?
What did we do?

Maybe this Christmas year could end up being
World War I or maybe next year could be II.
This Christmas is like those wars
Because parents have to give gifts
To their children this year,
And Covid is gonna make this hard.
It might be a lot of fights over presents.
Stores might have to ration.

Since Covid is coal,
It makes people sad.
You can hear or see
Random people crying.
Both make people sad.

The cure for Covid
Is almost here...
But is it almost like
Being good to avoid
Getting coal?

So maybe we should all start being safe,
And start being and doing good, too.
Because the two Grinches this year
Are Covid and Coal.

Micah Edwards

4 Faceless

I know I Am Invisible

Yudi Cano

When my eyes don't sparkle
As they did and no one notices,
When I try to talk about what
My heart holds that is hurt and
No one listens, I want to yell to
Get some attention but I would
Be asking for it, so what is there to
Hold? I can't ask for attention
Because somewhere in this world,
There is someone craving
My attention just as much as
I am waiting for theirs.

The Joke

Brooke Cumbee

The jokes you told,
The jokes I laughed at,
The jokes I thought were funny,
The jokes were corny but you made funny.

The way you laughed,
That tea kettle squeal.
When you would laugh and I would start laughing,
When I laughed till my throat hurt.

Still telling jokes.
Jokes not as good as yours.
Even though you didn't know I was laughing,
You were amazing when you
Didn't even know who I was.

My feelings for you are like
A volcano that is about to explode.

The Years

Micah Edwards

As your teenage years go on,
It feels as if you are just a person in a crowd.
Not a lot of people acknowledge the things you do,
Even though you feel you should be recognized.

The fact that other can be known for starting drama.
And all you get is for helping someone or doing
An extremely good deed is a moment of appreciation.

It feels as though you don't stand out for doing the
Things that others would be given a medal for.

To fear you are disposable and can easily be replaced.

Iris Gudrunardottir

Dark Crowded Room

Victoria Flores

Completely alone in a crowded room,
Unable to find friends inside.
Feeling the lack of interaction with people.
I don't belong here.

Waiting for someone to talk to me.
Just sitting around it the darkness.
Everyone is ignoring me.
I start walking.

Seeing students from school in the shadows.
Hearing sounds of laughter
As I walk down the hallway
And leave the dark crowded room.

Like A Floating Balloon

Victoria Flores

Alone during school,
My friends being absent.
Walking inside the classroom on my own.
Friends not beside me like usual.

The class seems so silent and grey.
I feel like a floating balloon
Just passing by hallways.
It's raining really hard.

Eating late lunch last,
Seats empty with no friends here.
I wish they would come back.
I see them the next day.

Ulises Oliva Tellez

People Walking By

Tyniece Graham

There's people walking by and they don't see me
But I don't complain,
Although it may seem lonely at times.
It doesn't bother me.

There's people walking by and they don't see me
But I won't fret.
I bet if I had money on me I wouldnt be invisible.
It doesn't matter.

There's people walking by but they don't see me.
I walk, and walk but…
Nobody, not even a "hello how are you doing."
I come home thinking that I would come to

An empty home.
But a little furry surprise is
At my door.
Finally noticed.

Whatever I Want

Ulises Oliva Tellez

I can do whatever I want.
These people can't see me
I am faceless,
But I don't wanna stay like this.

I can't talk to no one.
All I can do is pretend,
Talk to myself.
That is kinda weird, though.

I hope people can see me again
Or else imma go insane.
I don't wanna do that.
Maybe I'll just put on a mask
So I can be seen again.

Forever hurt
And forever scarred.

Iris Gudrunardottir

Disappear

Ulises Oliva Tellez

Did I disappear
Or are people just messing with me?
Are these people blind?
I'm right in front of them.

No way is this real right now.
Im calling them.
No answer.
Have they forgotten?

I can do anything I want.
People cant see me
And that's not ok.
Hope they remember me again.

Micah Edwards

Unseen

Cole Palzer

When people ignore you it starts to get annoying,
Because no one will listen to what you will say,
And everyone acts like they can't see you, when

You try to get help from other people and they ignore
You, you would most likely get mad since getting ignored
Is rude, for example when one of my classmates get

Done with school and goes to the library next to the
School, he mainly does homework in there, and when
He has a lot of homework he tries asking for help but

Everyone ignores Him, which makes him very mad
Since he can't get help, it will take longer for him to
Do his work.

Laying In Ruin

Jameson O. Perkins

I was tired of carrying it,
A burden worst than Hell itself.
I had to let it out,
I told almost everyone.

They didn't care.
One day I just broke.
During this I felt like I was being set free,
Then I felt as if a million nukes were going off.

I ended up passing out.
When I awoke I saw what had happened,
I saw cities laying in ruins,
Along with huge cross like beams of light.

I was living in my personal Hell.
One that I made.
All thanks to what was in me,
A weapon for killing gods.

Some And Others

Kaitlyn Williams

Some have all the friends in the world,
Others have one or two.

Some like being in the spotlight,
Others like sitting in the shadows.

Some tell jokes and people laugh,
Others tell jokes and nobody hears them.

Some ask and get answers,
Others ask questions and dont receive an answer.

Some dont get in trouble.
Others get blamed everytime.
Some say something once and are heard.
Others have been waiting years.

Some dont have to work and get rich or famous.
Others work their whole lives barely making it.

Some get noticed.
Others dont get a second glance.

Second Place

Kaitlyn WIlliams

"Second place is First place for losers."
Second place gets forgotten
Second place is just the dude that came next
The dude that crossed the finish line after the person.

Do you see any second place people in history books?
"1st black doctor."
"1st woman to vote."
"1st billionaire."

Nobody even remembers the second president.
We only talk about George Washington.
And he didn't even do anything for this country.
Now that I think about it, neither did the second president.

Nobody remembers second place.
They're forgotten and never talked about.
Thats why its called "Second Place."
It's a participation award, basically.

You're only the guy that came after the person
Everybody is talking about.
The person that won first place.
The person that beat you.

Wings

Hailee Gudrunardottir

I remember when I was younger. Because I had nothing to
Worry about, but, now that I'm older I've met reality. The
Real world is brutal. There is hate everywhere. It doesn't
Matter if you're perfect. They'll find a way. LGBTQ+ gets

A lot of hate because we are 'disobeying' God. Most people
Hide from it and feel invisible for it. I get nasty comments for
Liking the same gender people make fun of my sexuality for
It. I'm going to say that I don't care. It's my choice to love

People. No matter their looks, personality, or gender If you
Don't like it, then look away. If you're a part of LGBTQ+, and
You're scared of what'll happen to you. I'm going to tell you
That people's opinions don't matter. You'll soon learn to

Spread your wings and soar through the skies with us
There are always people out there to hurt you and others who
Will love you. Your friends support you. Your family supports
You. We all love and support you. Because you're someone

That will become a hero.

Olivia Summerlin

5 On Love And Hate

The Loop

Kamaria Bacon

As her heart has been broken,
She looks for others to pick up the pieces.
As she lives in a constant loop,
She keeps going back.

As the toxic ness runs through their veins,
She finally finds someone to keep
The pieces together
As they care for her like nobody

She has ever seen.
She can finally be happy.
She can finally have self-care.
She can finally leave the loop.

Was It Fun Choosing Her?

Aldrey Lopez

You make me angry
For not understanding my feelings.
All the afternoons waiting
For your text, "Hey!"

All the nights we stayed up
Till 5:00am playing Fortnight,
Texting like nothing else excited.
It's now all gone.

Maybe one day you'll realize
That you did me wrong.
I'll be waiting for that day.
I wonder if I can forgive you.

Was it fun choosing her?
Did she give you love like I did?
I hope you enjoy her.
I lost and you won.

Before You Know

Angela Gonzalez Gomez

It's been so long.
Hopefully i'll be gone before you know.
I hear your voice all night and day.
Sang our song until I drove away.

When saying "I love you" to someone.
You don't only have to say it.
You have to prove it
Or have to show it.
And have to mean it, by heart.

I'll go away if you want me to.
Won't take too long.
If we meet again,
Ill say goodbye to my love for you.
Why try?

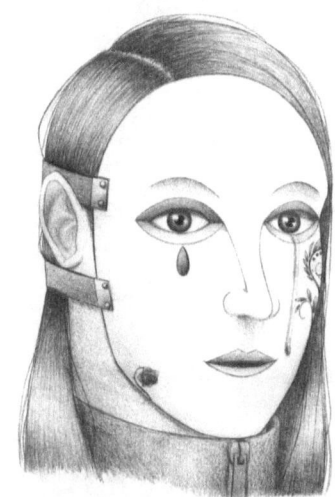

Alexis Bacani

Love Is A Waste Of Time

Monserrat Tinoco

Love is a waste of time.
At the end of the day, people will leave you.
Love is just a word.
Doesn't mean anything if they didn't mean it.

You can say I love you tell anyone.
You don't mean it because you are young.
Love is just fake, honestly.
Either they will leave your life
And still speak on your name.

People who are toxic don't love you.
They want to control and make you feel like nothing.
Also give you the most insecurities and not worth it.
They can just make you feel bad
About yourself and say they love you.

People these days don't mean love to anyone.
They say it just to make you happy.
Stop saying love to make someone happy, ha yeah.
Love would always drop you into depression.

Thanks To You

Aldrey Lopez

Thanks to you, I couldn't give him love.
He was different from you.
He actually cared for me.
He wasn't selfish.

You just gives me sadness.
He was there when I was sad.
He checked up on me
When you were with her.

Now neither you nor him are in my life.
I'll miss none of you.
I don't feel like taking y'all.
I deserve better as well as y'all.

Maybe we'll see each other
In the future, but not now.
Maybe we'll all change.
We had fun though.

Behind My Back

Monserrat Tinoco

Hate when people just be don't be direct.
Be straight up stop trying to talk behind my back.
How fake is that ha you thought you would be direct.
Come on say what you were gonna say.

Stop trying to be direct with your friends
If you aint bold enough to say it.
Just say it like it be making me mad,
Like ugh stop trying to get attention.

Try to sound cool or look at it.
It's not even worth it.
Just to be direct and throw shade at someone.
Stop being childish and already say it.

Being a little childish, he never saw me.
Clearly, thats you. Thats how you are .
Get attention make yourself,
Look dumb or whatever.
I know you are not direct either way.

Tell Me About You

Faydrya Williams

The time you had to tell me about you
Was the time I could have been eating.
The time I had try to tell you about me
Is the time you had to go.

The places I could have been screaming and yelling.
The times I could of been a waterfall.
But the true time was me helping you.
The time that was confusing and yet so clear.

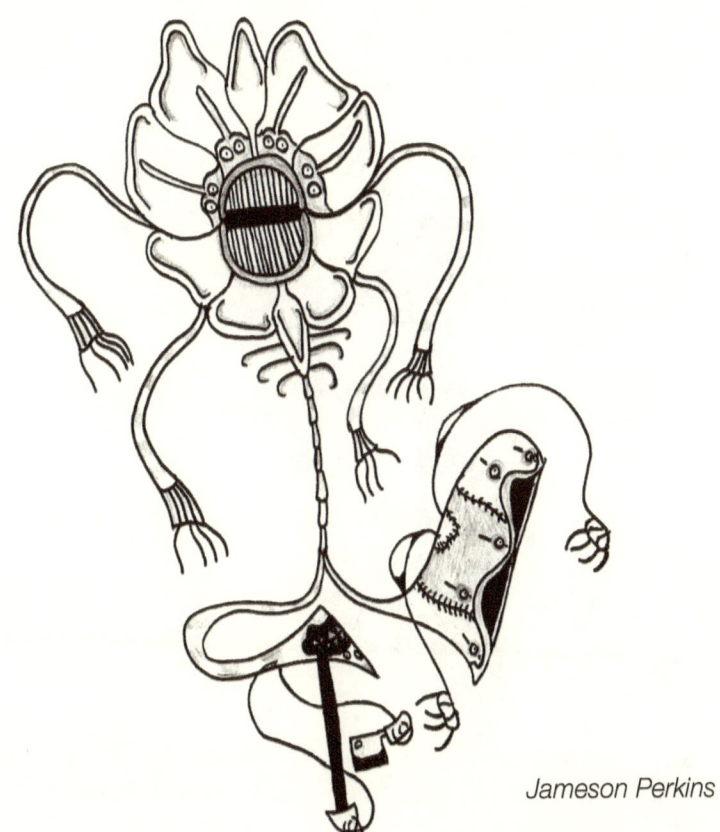

Jameson Perkins

Amor

Victoria Williams

Red like to bloom for me and you,
Dinner table filled with grape juice sweet,
My heart goes back and forth like yay,
Praises go down and up for tomorrow's day.

He will always be my star and sun.
The candle goes off for you in room.
Suitcase go suitcase come back like a heart.
Many go, many come, for I will love.

Jameson Perkins

An Exception

Vanessa Camacho Mendoza

I hate everyone and everything,
But you were an exception.
When you loved me,
I felt like I was free.

I didnt have to pretend to be someone i'm not.
Suddenly every romance book
Reminded me of you.
To me, you were my universe,
But to you I was a curse.

The Heartbreak

Jenifer Guerrero Perez

They first act like they love you.
They say they would be there for you.
And then one day they will be gone foreve.
And leave you with a broken heart.

And then expect you to be over it.
He once loved me and now I'm astranged.
As much as you did hurt me,
You did make me happy at one point in my life.

And all I can do now is just remember all the memories,
And think about all of our good moments.
As much as it hurts its worth to let that all go.
Now all that's left to do is to be happy without someone.

9.14.19

Ahmyah Jackson

Don't say you're going to be there forever
If you're just going to give up.
Don't say you're as loyal as a dog
If you're just as fake as fantasies.

Deep conversations and promises lead to
Time wasted. Boom! That's the sound
Of you breaking my heart.
Five months of wrapping a bandage

Around the heart you broke.
I hope karma treats you well,
What goes around comes around.

Nijayla Aiken

Together For Never

Aniyah Toomer

It started off like a fairytale romance.
We were inseparable like two peas in a pod.
Never apart for too long,
Our love was so strong.

It all started to crumble
When our parents found out,
Trying to keep us apart.
A love forever gone but never forgotten.

Playa, Playa

Ahmyah Jackson

The whole time, you used me as a tool.
Useful when you needed me, useless when you didn't.
Gave you my all, but you made me fall.
Trust and love turned to rust and lust.

The empire we had burned like fire.
Good times turned into bad times.
Not wanting to fight and fuss
just wanting to make it right.

Heartbreak

Aniyah Toomer

Pain in one's heart is not a good feeling,
Hurt is an emotion that brings so much despair
Will it ever go away?
It is too much to bear.

The feeling of love has you flying like the birds
Finding that special someone settles your nerves,
Long walks and wine,
Are also devine.

Ride Or Die

Ahmyah Jackson

Don't act like I didn't care.
Don't act like I didn't love you.
When you're lying and denying
Telling people we didn't have anything.

Telling them about the late conversations.
The hours of being on the phone together.
I've always been the rider,
You just weren't the right driver.

Broken

Juelz Ultreras Segundo

You broke my heart.
It is shattered into pieces,
Like stepping on a cheerio.
It's gone, it's irreparable.

I'm only left with the remnants
Of a broken heart
Waiting to be repaired,
But that's not possible.

I used to be full.
Now Im empty.
Empty as a box,
With nothing to fill it.

I think of you everyday,
Thinking of the good times.
I wish we could be together,
But that is now the past.

Lovesick

Hailee Gudrunardottir

My heart trapped
In an endless hallway of heartbreak.
Will it ever stop?
The pain is unbearable.

You left me here in the cold,
Leaving me to the darkness
To forever fall in a pit of sadness.
But why do I keep doing it?

I was meant to be alone.
I was born to be alone.
We were born to be alone
But why are we still looking for love?

Lexie Summerlin

It Sucks

Kaitlyn Williams

Guys will say anything to your face
Just to get you back to his place.

He'll talk about your eyes so blue
In the end, he breaks your heart into two.

They'll tell you that they care
Only to see you in your underwear.

You think, "Maybe, just maybe."
Then 9-months later, you end up with a baby.

Ashley Sanders

Kiss Love Goodbye

Hailee Gudrunardottir

Love.
"The strongest force in the galaxy."
Ha! What a joke.
Love isn't great.
Love can tear you down in seconds.

"Why do you have to be such a downer?"

I'm just speaking the truth.
People can give you gifts and tell you
That they "love you." Next thing you know,
You're burning every single memory of them.

You can still love people, but just be careful.
Humans are unpredictable.
They can turn on you in minutes,
But they can make you feel pain in seconds.

I Want To Be Loved

Yudi Cano

I want to be loved like
The moons loves the sun.
I want to be held like a
Mother holding her child.
I want to be adored like when
Clouds watch birds as they soar.
I want to feel safe, like two
Dewdrops when they're bubbled
On top of daffodil leaves.
Sleeping underneath the willow tree,
I want to feel complete.

Kaleah Jones

Come Back

Brooke Cumbee

You choose to come back,
Hoping to walk into my heart again
Like you never left, or I say shattered it
Like you made me feel like I was worthless.

It is the way I made you feel,
Or the times we had together,
Or it is that I wanted you to come back,
Or is it that I smile when I see you?

The thing I know is that I won't fall for you again.
I will never fall in love with you again.
I will never think of you the way I used to think of you.
I will not love you ever again.

But He Did Not

Angela Gonzalez

She stayed loyal, but he did not.
She waited for him in the good
And bad days, but he did not.
She gave him her heart, but he broke it apart.

You had to of been confused I am also
Confused. Can we get things straight?
But no, you dared to leave it like this
Without telling me and now, I am here lost.

Dealing With Heartbreaks

Maria Garcia

Going through a heartbreak is hard.
People always handle them differently.
Some people might cry for days or they go out instead.
Others use them as a lesson.
The experiences let people know what to do or not do
Boys and girls should know how to not take
Things too seriously.
They should also be aware of the
Things that could happen, getting over someone
Or dealing with a broken heart is
Not easy but it's not impossible.

Love

Maria Garcia

Love is like the wind, it comes and goes.
Not everything is forever and we have to understand that
There is sometimes strong or weak air, like feelings.
Things work out when there's a strong
Connection between both people.

As time passes by, those feelings might change.
Some might lose them of others might grow more.
Getting too attached though is not good.
Things will always change.

Come Back

Iyana Gayle

Walking down the steps
With depression written on my face,
I loved him with all I had,
But alas it wasn't enough to keep him in place,

Right where I wanted him when I needed him,
He left without a trace.
Now I sit around and mope
As tears flow down my cheeks.
Why, Why did you leave me?

The One

Marlene Gonzalez

You met the one,
You know they're the person you've been waiting for
You knew the instant you met.
It hit as fast as a bullet
They have hit the bullseye to your heart
This is what others meant by
Knowing when you met the one
It hits, next thing you know
You're planning your life with them.
They make you smile like a maniac.

Barf. Love.

Teandra Johnson

Once had some friends who dated each other
They were two completely different people.
The only reason they were dating, honestly
Was just because of me, the third-wheeler.

Both were best friends of mine, who I was with 24/7.
Was I suppose to know they were going to suddenly date?
You could barely even notice I was the odd one out.
They weren't even together unless I was also present.

Never See It Coming

Mahogony Hollington

Why do people get in their feelings all the time?
Why do they let their emotions take over them?
Why do they wear their hearts on their sleeves
For the world to know?
And why when they get their heart broken
They cry like they never see it coming?

Love is young,
Love is old,
Love is like an unwanted guest
showing up at your doorstep,
And yet we welcome it in.

Love is annoying,
With love comes heartbreak,
Love is never boring,
With it come feelings, drama,
And unwanted people

Love is like flipping a coin,
There are two sides to choose from,
Only they choose you,
You never know which side your going to end up with,
You just know, you have to put up with it.

Alone Till Further Notice

Teandra Johnson

Dating doesn't sound fun at all.
My sister dated the "hot" quarterback at Stall.
They've broken up a bazillion times for the past years.
Such a useless relationship bringing nothing but tears.

People make it seem like the greatest thing ever.
Others end up in a bad place with trauma forever.
I hereby stand that dating is pretty pointless.
I'd rather be alone till further notice.

2021 Relationships

Kaleah Jones

We feel this connection;
The strong attachment that is hard to let go.
The urge to do everything together.
We fell in love.

Now things are different.
You feel like you're ten miles away,
Wondering why you're left in the dark,
Begging for something to fix what you have lost.

Teenage Loverboy

Angel Perez

Oh Dear.
May you seem like everything in the world.
Lit like a spark in the darkness,
For you are the spark that lit my world up.

Before you,
Reality seemed corrupt.
And after you,
It will be tough.

For if you leave,
I would want to stay in this forsaken dream.
Life crumbles at its seams.
Nothing will be the same.

For you will cause me to tear.
Oh Dear.

Love

Mia Trejo

I never thought love could cause pain,
Especially if you're not even dating.
I just can't explain
How my heart is aching.

Always being second choice.
How much it hurts
Knowing you can't avoid,
That you are worse.

My Soulmate?

Kaleah Jones

When you left I was broken.
I had nothing left but pain and memories.
I thought that you were the one for the future.
Hoping that we would've made something together,
Wondering if I'll ever see you again.

We both had our issues to work through.
Some that can be fixed so that we'll meet again.
All that replays is your voice in my head,
Missing the feeling of being loved,
Maybe we weren't meant to be.

Glass Shards

Angel Perez

Why did you leave?
Left me in the wind to make me bleed.
Use those words as glass shards,
Cut my love for you into pieces.

I would have done anything for you.
Sacrifice if it was a need.
But at last, you left me.
Now I am gone like the wind.

Him

Mia Trejo

His green eyes .
So pretty, like a garden.
I could stare at them for hours.
I love him.

The way he makes me feel safe,
Like all the hate in the world is gone.
When I'm with him everything goes away.
I love him.

The Boy Named A

Mia Trejo

He was so nice,
But I had to say no.
What was the price?
I didn't know.

Losing a friend,
He still doesn't know.
Why did it have to end?
I still love him, though.

Why not me?

Mia Trejo

Is it weird what I'm feeling?
I don't love her, do I?
Why do I have to be dealing
With this weird feeling that I can't deny?

I love her.
But why?
We were just friends, but now
I want to cry

All We Do

Ulises Oliva Tellez

All we do is love each other,
But we also hate one another.
We have friendly, lovely talks,
But we also scream and argue.

We have cuddles.
We hit each other.
Saying I love you.
Surprisingly saying I hate you.

Same things happen
We start loving and hating
All this begins by waking up in the morning
All this ends with a good night sleep

Kamaria Bacon

A Bitter Goodbye

Hailee Gudrunardottir

Is this it? Is it really over?
It can't be. Not like this

We've been by each other's side for so long
And this is what I get
Pain and suffering because of something you did
And I thought we were a team

We fought together, we cried together,
We argued, hugged, and laughed together.
And now you want to leave all of that behind?

Well, I wish you the best. You always were a friend to me.
I'm sorry if I wasn't enough for you. I never am to anyone.

I just want you to know that
I care about you deeply.
And that I hope you can forgive my sins one day.
Please, I know I've messed up.

Enough talking.
I'll miss you, buddy.
I know you're doing it for your own good.
So long, friend.

It'll be okay

Hailee Gudrunardottir

We all want to be loved.
Some people don't know it yet.
I'm going to lay some truth onto you, and I'm sincere.

I've had my fair share of love.
Most of them never ended well.
I've been cheated on,
And my heart's been broken a few times.

But, this relationship is unique.
Something that no one has had
They want to be with you
They care about you

Just know that everything will be okay
Your friends are here to support you
We all love you, and that's what matters
We are your family

Just stay by their side. They need you in their life.
You make them stronger. You make them powerful.
You are someone they love, someone they want to marry.
Someone who they care about,
And if they hurt you, then move on.

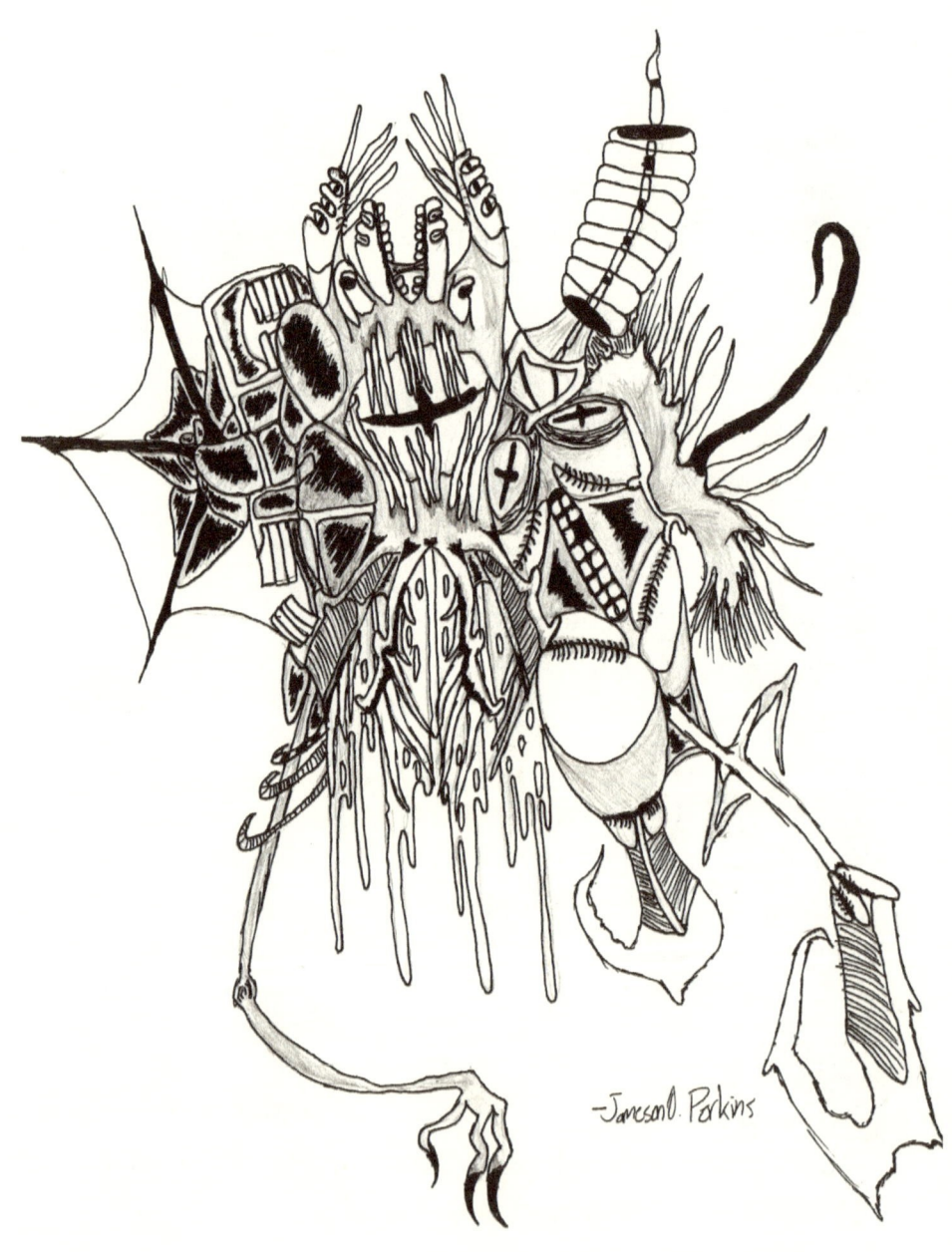

Jameson Perkins

6 Sorry, Not Sorry

For Being Different

Yudi Cano

For being different and acting different
I am too in love with myself, to care of
What you think. Because when
I try to fit in your standards of beauty,

I felt in my hearts this wasn't
My beauty but your's,
So sorry not sorry for being
My own kind of beauty.

Filters

Brook Cumbee

I use filters every day of the year.
I am not talking about using picture filters,
But personality filters every day.
This happens everyday for so many people.

I am not sorry for the filter I use.
The filters add confidence.
The filters add self-esteem or more personality.
Anything that I have done wrong.

The filters add anything you need.
It is has become automatic to add filters.
Even if the filters change small things,
The filters add small to the big change that is needed.

They can change personalities.
They will change you.
They can change the way you look at yourself.
They will change the way you see yourself.

Not Feeling Sorry

Victoria Flores

Sitting in the daylight,
I look up at the window,
Thinking all about those conversations we had,
Not feeling sorry for all I said to them.

Getting painful memories
As I remember inch by inch,
Muttering to myself,
"Hah, they mustn't have cared."

The feeling was cold and harsh.
PLOP! PLOP!
Tears started to sting my eyes,
And some never-ending cries.

In defiance of the capitol, Katniss and Peeta try and kill themselves so that there is no winner of the Hunger Games.

Lexie Summerlin

I Don't Like People

Angela Gonzalez

I don't like people who are childish.
They can be sorry for me cause I did
Something wrong, but I'm not sorry for
Them for getting something wrong.

Sorry for not talking to you.
Sorry for being rude to you.
Sorry for what I have done to you,
But I'm not sorry for you leaving me.

Getting In The Way

Victoria Flores

Things were getting in the way,
As the days pass by.
Life is so lonely and quiet.
It must not like me.

I'm Not Sorry

Tyniece Graham

I'm not sorry for eating my sisters chicken.
She asked where it was and I said, "I don't know."
But even though I'm not sorry,
I still don't want to stand up and admit it.

I told my sister I ate her chicken.
She was mad but understood.
But she told me if i ate it again,
I would wake up without an art book.

I ate another one of her chickens and I wasn't sorry.
But the next morning, I woke up with no book.
I asked my sister if she had taken my art book.
But she said, "No, I was just playin."

Then I saw my little sister drawing all over my art book.
My sister said that It was karma, and
She wanted me to apologize,
But guess what? I was never sorry.

Strangers With Candy

Learric Green

Whoops I missed the halloween trick or treating.
I was going to go but time just flies by so fast.
Probably because of some games and tv shows,
But I was looking forward to this,well kinda at least.

Got a costume but none was needed for that day.
Had to walk somewhere to get picked up
Across the street, kinda far if you ask me.

Time flew. Had on nothing except the tv.
Forgot about the costume and the plans,
But I think I had more fun at home than getting
Candy from strangers down the street.

They Get Mad

Scarlett Santiago

You talk bad about my friends,
I'll talk back.
Push my friends,
I will push back.
Mess with my friends,
Mess with me.

My sister steasl my charger,
I take it back.
They take it again.
I get mad, they get mad.
It's dumb.

Jayden Snipe

What's The Point?

Monserrat Tinoco

What's the point, honestly?
Kids still wont listen regardless
If you write them up.
They won't listen to the
Dress code because its dumb.
We will still wear anything.
The boys will still have their pants down.

Some parents can't afford the uniform
For their kids so they struggle.
Kids have to wear the uniform until highschool.
They get tired of wearing the same thing
Over and over.

Kids don't care about what
The teacher tells them about their clothes.
Call home, they think, it's just a waste of time.
Who knows why we don't like it?

They want to be comfortable.
We want to feel like if we were at home,
Even if its only for a year.
The uniforms are just uncomfortable.

LGBTQ,+, I Don't Care

Hailee Gudrunardottir

Yeah, yeah, I've heard it before.
"Being gay is a sin!"
"You are going to Hell!"
"How dare you disobey God like that?!"

Yeah, I don't care.
I'm happy of being who I am.
I don't need your lousy opinion
That no one really asked for.

If you want to find someone
Who wants to listen to your opinions,
There's a wall right over there.
Have fun with it!

Micah Edwards

Let People See

Monserrat Tinoco

People who cry ugh just be getting a lot of attention
Don't be crying in front of people, that
Makes you look soft and lowkey dumb
Cause you're letting people know
You cry and let people see.

Makes people wonder what you are
If you cry you seem like a baby.
Its showing your weakness.
It's embarrassing to cry.

People would know that you cry easily.
Everyone would know you got a soft spot.
Make you feel less to yourself.
Kids will make fun of you.

Crying makes you feel vulnerability.
Lets people know what your emotions are.
Have an idea what you go through in daily basis.
Start assuming things about you.

Applesauce On The Table

Ulises Oliva Tellez

I saw applesauce on the table.
Wonder who's that could be?
Oh well, I'm eating it.
Down the hatch.

He comes in,
Wondering who ate his food.
He asks, "Who ate it?"
I say, "Me. I did.

It looked delicious.
Forgive me,
But I don't care.
I'm sorry, not sorry."

Lexie Summerlin

Going To Ashley

Mark Chavez

Going to Ashley,
Leaving everyone behind.
Going to be alone.
Going to West Ashley.
Some say the ghetto.

Nothing can go wrong,
But everything can.
No help, just alone.
Alone but pushed to the limit.

April Fools Day

Ulises Oliva Tellez

April fools day.
Time for some pranks, I say.
Lets see if someone faints.

Setting up the prank. No biggie.
All done by the end of the day.
Someone is about to play.

He walks up and gets scared
Scared to death . He asks why
I say I'm sorry. but I'm not sorry.

Don't Be An Idiot

Maily Martinez Martinez

I'm not sorry to feel this way.
You made me feel this way your own.
You made me mad and cold.
Now you cant change me,
So don't try.

Don't be nasty and ugly,
Don't be an idiot.
I guess my name tasted good,
Because it's always in your mouth.

I guess I have also told you bad things,
But don't be dumb and stop wasting your time on me.
I guess I look innocent,
But that doesn't make me innocent.

The One God

Jameson O. Perkins

What would you feel if you were
Forced to quit your normal life,
What about saying bye to what you love,
Being forced to leave the
Others who don't believe.
Tricked into being robbed of opportunities,
And being told you would
Die and then learn everything.

All others would burn in the depths of hell.
While others were given a chance to learn.
Forced to hide because of your own beliefs,
This is what the witness is.

Nothing but brainwashing,
People controlling,
Gathering, and
Repeating.
The process
Just repeats itself.

Identity

Hailee Gudrunardottir

I am African American.
I am Asian.
I am Hispanic.
I am me.

Just because we're a different color than you,
That doesn't mean we're a threat to anyone.
You are just being childish,
And no one enjoys your tantrums.

You can't change us.
We're staying here.
And you can't do anything about it.
And I'm not sorry about that.

Mahogony Hollington

Left Them

Learric Green

Didn't mean to leave them there.
At least, not at first.
I was suppose to go outside, see the fresh air.
But couches are comfy.

I said I would be there
But that was a small chance.
I'm so sad that I missed the party,
But I didn't miss my favorite show.

I didn't want to go out there.
I didn't need to go out there.
Said I would be but wasn't.
I think I made a choice that was better for me.

I was controlling what
I wanted to do and I did it.
I stayed in like I wanted.
Did what I wanted.

Why School?

Juelz Ultreras Segundo

Why school?
So boring and so unnecessary.
Minutes feel like hours and hours feel like days.
I wish I could escape
And never come again.

If I could decide
I would get rid of school.
School is not fun
And I will not apologize.

Masks

Juels Ultreras Segundo

Masks should not be required
They make it hard to breathe
Each person has a decision,
Each person has a choice.

If you don't feel it being necessary,
You shouldn't be obligated to wear it.
It's not an obligation
It's a safety measurement.

Flowers And Rainbows

Emma Daley

Teenage angst is the realization that
Everything isn't flowers and rainbows.
The realization that not everything
Can be solved with friendship and words.
That the world we face isn't perfect.
That alone can destroy a person.

Becoming an adult is deciding
What you'll do about that evil.
Whether you decide to keep quiet
And get an office job, or do the opposite.
Those before us chose to keep quiet.
The evil is just now getting

The attention it deserves.
It's not anyone else's fault but
yours if you cannot adapt your mind.
Adaptation is the key to survival.

Micah Edwards

Religion

Emma Daley

Religion is something people
In this world rely on.
Don't twist my words, people have
The right to express their own
Beliefs and I support that.
But why do we so easily allow

These beliefs and rights to
Control everything?
Separation of church and state.
Yet those on top of the hill still
Justify everything through the belief in god.

I do not care what you believe in.
You are purposely harming people,
Justifying it by words in a book.
How should I trust a god that
justifies so much hate in this world?
Justifies the unlawful killing of so many...

Pineapple

Maria Garcia

I think that pineapple does not belong on pizza.
Girls don't always have to wear skirts and dresses.
Everyone has their own style,
But she thinks differently.

Pineapple pizza is her favorite.
She thinks that dresses and heels
Are a must-have for girls.
Style defines who you are.
Everyone has their own opinions.

Cry, Babies

Sydney Garcia

Everyone looked forward to the future.
Thoughts of computers, phones, and more.
But with living in the 21st century,
You begin to notice lots of sensitivity.

Cartoons get "canceled."
Petitions are created.
Jokes aren't made
Because hypersensitivity seems
Common these days.

Rhythm & Blues

Sydney Garcia

The world stops for nobody.
It's cruel and unfair.
A den for liars, cheaters, and thieves,
But that's just the way it is.

You aren't entitled to anything in life.
People owe you nothing.
Not even a simple hello on the street.
That's how it is and always will be.

I Believe

Marlene Gonzalez

I believe women should be able to
Choose their spouses in every place.
I believe women should have an
Education in all places.
I believe women should have equal
Opportunities for jobs as men.
I believe women should be treated equally as men
It isn't always the case but should be.
Everyone is equal and that should be shown.
There shouldn't be stereotypes involving
Gender or anything. Everyone is their own
Person and shouldn't change for that.

All In The Past

Mahogony Hollington

I'm not sorry that I spoke my mind.
I'm not sorry you are mad.
You'll get over it.
It's all in the past.

I will not apologize for not being respectful.
I know what I want,
You know what I want,
You're just avoiding the topic.

Did you really think I wouldn't find out?
Stop acting innocent.
We both know what's going on.
We both know how to solve it.

I'm not mad at you,
I'm just not sorry.
You had your chance.
You didn't use it.

Rules To Grasp

Teandra Johnson

Society has too many rules to grasp,
Makes it hard to have any fun.
A new generation puts it all in the past,
The old ones try to take them back like an obsession.

Why do people even care anymore?
Let whoever be who they wanna be!
A happier future is what's in store,
Just let those dumb rules finally fly free.

Dress-Code Is A No Go

Teandra Johnson

Outfits here and some clothes there!
Which idiot gave them genders?
Take those away and now it's fair!
Just ignore all those annoying bickers!

The whole world was never always like this,
Separation of boy-girl wasn't a constant pursuit.
But we can fix it up so all genders can wear a dress!
Go on and rock that nice tuxedo suit!

I'm Not Apologizing

Kaleah Jones

The police are biased.
Detaining people based off skin color.
Hurting families.
Creating chaos.

Making people second guess
Why they're a target.
Everyone is equal.
Nobody should feel less
Than what they are.
The police is biased.

Be Yourself

Kaleah Jones

We all love someone,
Same or different.
The connection between you is realistic.
Apologizing for who you love is pessimistic.

Love who you love
Knowing doubt will come.
But all that matters is you love who you love.
We all love someone.

I'm Not Sorry

Brooke Cumbee

I'm not sorry for the things I said.
I'm not sorry for the things I did.
I'm not sorry for the way I treated you.
Because you are not sorry, either.

You are not sorry for the things you said.
You are not sorry for the things you did.
You are not sorry for the things
You made me do to other people.
You are not sorry for the things
You made me say to other people.

You said things that cause this.
You did things to me that made me do it.
You caused this all to happen.
It was your fault.

Micah Edwards

Angela Gomez

7 Five By Seven By Five

Mark Chavez

There is no justice
The world is falling apart
There could be a exit

Want to fall asleep
Stay awake or grades will tank
Too much work to sleep

Ariana Amador

A regular day
George Floyd was shot by police
Minneapolis

Normal day routine
She was shot in her apartment
Breonna was young

Now protests begin
Black lives matter protesters
We want some justice

Victoria Williams

Justice everywhere
Makes me so happy all day
I can get so much

How is my heart beat
For it is always equal
Justice shall be here

Have no fear, in heart
For justice is here always
Will always be here

Universe awake
Justice we can always have
I like it a lot

Coronavirus
Makes me very mad all-day
I do not like it

Mask on,at all times
Coronavirus is blown up
I got my nose covered

Tick tock to the mask
We all know we don't have plans
Corona got demands

Have no fear, in heart
For justice is here always
Will always be here

Mask free I don't see
I am very unhappy
Covid is boring

Corona disease
I do not want to be there
It feels like it burns

Ruby Cedillo

No equal treatment.
Standing up for those in need.
When others will not

Big round bright red cheeks.
The skin color of the big sun.
Pikachu he says.

No sympathy shown.
Authorities are biased.
True colors are shown.

Fear of waking up.
Walking down a street, heartbeats.
Streets filled with sorrow.

Soft fluffy gray fur.
Round eyes filled with adventure.
Paws gentle and sweet.

Room with witnesses.
Enemy across from you.
Justice must be served.

Her hair is long and smooth.
Her smile is perfect and unique.
Everything special

We want equal treatment.
Deaths of innocent people.
No one left behind.

Jaylne Manigault

I need my justice
We need a better system
I don't understand

Justice was not shown
They weren't on my side at all
I was left to die

No sympathy shown.
Authorities are biased.
True colors are shown.

Justice was not served
I can't take it anymore
I am sick of this

Where has justice gone
It's like they don't work for us
I have to try hard

I am now so tired
They won't even look at me
This ain't right at all

Let's break it down now
Please let's tear down the system
Let's get our justice

Kevin Saucedo Contreras

Do all lives matter?
Nah bro you trippin yo head
Black lives do matter

The shots firing
Cops can't keep calm and chill out
Them bullets hurt us

People protesting
Leave the people alone
Just stop killing them

Mobs are going mad
All this is extremely sad
One life gone caused this

Why do they do this
They just kill for no reason
Just leave them alone

The Parkland shooting
Nikolas cruz aint get shot
But some people do

The kids in cages
Detached from their parents
Trapped out like dogs

Rashida Frasier

Communities gone
Bullets with no names are real
Families broken

Spiders crawling near
Uncomfortable and scared
I want my mommy

Liars in the tall seat
Black and brown not welcome here
Corrupted new name

I wonder when my
breaking comes; the trust-breaking.
One day justice reigns

Hi I am U.S
We lie in our media
We kill but blame china

My morals standstill,
As I push for redemption,
my conscience confused.

Ahyah Jackson

Minding his business
Policemen wanted to kill
Living being black

Phobias are lame
Making people scared of things
Having fears of heights

Resting in the night
Breonna Taylor was killed
By police "protecting"

Do not be depressed
Or sad about anything because
It's almost Friday

Kids getting bullied
Just want to have a good day
Stop the bullying

Mentally challenged
Daniel Prude died by some gunshot
Police are killing

Asleep in his car
By police brutality
Rayshad Brooks got killed

Mia Mccoy

Black lives do matter
We need justice in this world
This is very unfair

We fight for our right
We want peace and equality
We march for our right

Brown dogs are so cute
They have so much fluffy fur
I want a dog badly

Everyone needs justice
This world is falling apart
Everyone is going crazy

I like pink ice cream
Especially the rainbow
I like the cone shape

This world needs fixing
Everyone needs to take chill pills
Violence isn't good

I like to color
Coloring books with dogs are cool
I like bright colors

We need change today
A change to make everyone agree
Start changing today

Devin Pinckney

We fight for justice
If no justice then no peace
We cry out for peace

Justice more than peace.
Peace first then become justice.
No justice, no peace.

Justice and the peace
We fight for peace and justice
We don't get neither.

We will fight for peace
If justice, why would we fight?
We would fight for peace

We fight for justice
If it's peace why would we fight?
We fight for justice

Aniyah Toomer

Violence everywhere
People trashing the building
People getting hurt

A sit-in to start
Rosa Parks makes history
Segregation ends

Police not caring
People marching down the street
Buildings burning down

Martin Luther King
Organized marches to help
Peaceful protesting

Started out peaceful
It quickly became violent
No justice no peace

Going to the store
Loved ones never coming back
Justice should be served

Is my home safe now?
Police kicking in your door
Breonna Taylor

Zyera Brown

What is justice? Is
Justice color of the skin?
There is no justice.

This isn't justice.
Justice is not what this is.
Being in the fear.

Is there any justice?
When will change ever happen?
Make some change happen.

Beaten and stomped
Is violence their only option?
Violence is justice.

Where is the justice
Breonna Taylor is gone now
Where is her justice?

Standing on the neck
Until his very last breath
George Floyd.

Jovany Contreras

Pow shots fired at me
Shoot me once i'll get back up
I still died for you

Knee on his poor head
Him suffocating to death
George Floyd died with pain

Burning buildings down
Police shooting at people
Chaos is out there

Gas bombs thrown at us
We stay strong and fight back hard
We struggle to live

People rioting
The Capital door breaking
People rush inside

Avaree Fludd

Justice is a fight
A black and white, right and wrong
Someone dying young

Nonexistent Justice
Micheal Brown, Breonna Taylor
George Floyd, many others, gone

Always left for dead
Always shooting for the head
Always look ahead

Justice for you, but
No more Justice for you. Why?
Because you are brown

Micheal Brown was left
In a lonely street, for hours
Because they said no.

Lives, gone with the wind
A long lost verse for one's that
Did not make it home

Breonna Taylor,
Killed because they said why not?
Because she was free.

Awareness is here
Awareness for the ones we
Lost, brutally, killed

Jameson Perkins

8 Freestyling

What Did You Egg-spect?

Hailee Gudrunardottir

I'm not for yolks.
I don't make people crack up much,
So, don't get too egg-cited
Because I don't shell out.

Get ready!
My yolks are hard to egg-nore.
It's time to eggs-plore,
So grab an eggs-presso.

Actually, nevermind.
I'm eggs-hausted.
It's not an eggs-aggregation either.
Let's continue on Fry-day.

The Legend Of Aurora

Tristan Youngblood

Through all of Aurora, he spreads fear and pain
Though many others endure and train.
He instills panic and fright,
However, these few people shall stand and fight.

These people are now Ghosts,
And they are much braver than most.
This man is known as Walker
And to the Ghosts, he is a stalker.

My Happiness

Maily Martinez

Watching them is my happiness.
They teach me new things every day.
They say, "love yourself."
I say "I'm starting to love myself."
Now I see how beautiful I am.
Now I know "life goes on,"
No matter what, my "life goes on."
Now I'm someone who loves herself so much.
I wake up and think about how much I have changed
I see myself as a different person now
I realize what a good person I am
But I'm still learning how to myself
I still want to change things in me
But I won't stop till I love myself all the way.

Monserrat Tinoco

It's Time To Crack Up

Hailee Gudrunardottir

Welcome back, my little chicks!
I hope you had an egg-stravagant week.
Because it's now Fry-day,
And it's time to cracking.

It's time to tell a yolk.
It might be bad,
But I'm going to whisk it.
Here it goes…
Knock Knock…
(Who's there?)
Orange.
(Orange who?)

Orange, you glad you listened to this
Egg-splosive comedic poem?
This poem was egg-ceptional,
But, this group really poaches my best yolks.
Until we meet again!

Random Thoughts Going Through My Head

Alex Ramos

What would dogs look like if
They had human traits?
If cats ate human food and mice
Played with cats while
Elephants raced cows?

What would it feel like to be played
As punishment for being a player?
Why can't snakes and mice get along?
What would it be like to have a friendly world,
With no bullies, dangerous animals, or hurting animals?

What would it be like if everyone had the same lifestyle?
Same traits, no racism, or discrimination?
Karen free, No covid or any other disease?
If everyone liked you for who you are,
And everyone would be your friend,
Non-toxic relationships or friends,
Where we would all be flawless?

Would we all be happier?

African American

Kaitlyn Williams

I am African American.
My life is not as easy as you may think.

I am running a race with more hurdles.
I am playing the piano and you're playing the drums.

I am 3.23 times more likely to get shot by the police.
I am 5 times more likely to get arrested for a "crime."

I have to get a good education.
Otherwise, I won't be able to fend for myself.

I am an African American.
Because I am marching for others
Who have died fighting for what I'm fighting for.

I am an African American.
Because I've seen younger children ask
Police officers "Are you going to shoot us?"

I am an African American.
Because no white person could relate
To what I have to go through.

I am an African American.
Because I have to have proof so
I don't get in trouble.

It's not easy going out every day and
Having the fear that you might get shot.

It's not easy knowing that someone of your race
Is dying at the hands of people that are
Supposed to protect us.

And it's not easy knowing that some people
Value their life over others because of
the color of their skin.

The World

Learric Green

When I was still in elementary school,
The world looked so clean.
It looked like it had no type of evil
Walking on the same giant rock.
The trees and rocks shined under the sunlight.
The clouds glowed like they contained a
Little bit of light inside them.

The sky a bright and young blue color,
But now the sky is filled with smoke.
Trees cut down removing some animals' homes,
Litter everywhere ,on the ground. even next to a trash can.
Fires burning down everything.

A new virus making people lock away
The outside world. Faces have to be hidden.
Smiles erased.

Money changes

Javier Green

It changes some people.
Brings out some people personalities.
Makes people love you
That didn't love you before.

Money makes
People who didn't care about you
Care about you now.
Start caring when you get money.
But before you had money, they act like
They didn't know you.
They act like they didn't care about you.

Money makes
People ask you for money,
But wouldn't give you a penny.
They wouldn't even give you anything
To eat if you were starving.
Then when you give them enough money,
They run away with it
And never talk to you again

Game Master

Hailee Gudrunardottir

Your love is a game
Like there isn't a winner.
You wanna play these kinds of games?
Don't include me in it.

I have a better life to get to.
I don't need your pity for me.
Sure, my heart has been broken a couple of times,
But my heart knows what's best for me.

Your love will zoom right past,
And I won't be the one to catch it.
If only you truly loved someone,
Maybe they'll get it?

Nevaeh Chaplin

If you really want me,
You should've acted like it.
You hide your emotions,
So I wouldn't know.

But, for right now,
You're not worth it.
I suggest you walk away,
Before the embarrassment hits you.

I have my own path I'm walking
I'm leaving all my troubles behind
And yet you want to follow
Do you still believe that you're mine?

Nevaeh Chaplin

Games

Jameson O. Perkins

There's a lot of them that we like,
People love them. They play them,
A few are harder than all the other,

Yet we still play them.
It brings back memories. Some good,
And some bad,
No one can't say that they are stupid,

They make life just a bit funner.
They make people upset too.
That's okay though,
That's why we love the games.
That why they're made.
For people to enjoy.

Hesitant She Stands

Emma Daley

Hesitant, she stands.
One wrong move, in white mens eyes
She'll be named "guilty."

Let me see your hands.
Bam! Left dead on the pavement.
Sorry, they "looked suspicious."

Signs, crowds, union, peace?
The people shout for justice.
A young girl screaming.

Remain impartial.
An unbiased decision, fair
Fair skin, privilege.

Justice to all, all
People with the riches, all
People not deemed black.

The Legend Of Aurora - The Epic

Tristan Youngblood

Through all of Aurora, he spreads fear and pain
Though many others endure and train.
He instills panic and fright,
However, these few people shall stand and fight.

These people are now Ghosts,
And they are much braver than most.
This man is known as Walker
And to the Ghosts, he is a stalker.

He prowls the woods at night,
But his influence is finite.
Though the Ghosts make great attacks,
He always has a plan to come back.

Nevaeh Chaplin

He looked like a fish out of water
They took him to the slaughter
A marriage counselor files for divorce
The course for me is a marathon for you
I pursue the ghost that haunts me
It haunts me as if I were dead

I feel alive today
The prey of today is unclear
Unclear like someone looking at a solar eclipse
The microchips of today are the DVD of tomorrow
Tomorrow is today like today is tomorrow
My thoughts are unclear

Nevaeh Chaplin

IDOL

Hailee Gudrunardottir

You can call me a celebrity.
You can call me famous.
But, you can't put me down,
Or degrade me as you do to others.

No matter what, I will still respect you,
Even if you have flaws.
I won't judge you,
But you can't stop me from shining through.

In life, you are an Idol to someone.
Let them shine too.
Spread your wings and seize the night,
Letting the wind beneath your wings lift you higher.

Nijayla Aiken

You Can't See Me

Kaitlyn Williams

You can't see my smile.
You cant see my face.

You can only see
That I'm a different race.

Voice

Kaitlyn Williams

They expect us not to reply.
They tell me not to speak.
I am to be seen and not heard.
I have my own voice.
I speak when I need to.
I'll yell.
I'll scream.
I'll cry.
If that's what it takes for me to be heard.

Garden

Hailee Gudrunardottir

A life full of lies, a garden full of thorns.
When will it end?
This garden is full enough with
Loneliness and tears.

Now I know that I won't be able to fill this garden
Full of flowers and roses.
Giving this ruin some light, some color
Some love, some happiness.

What I know is that you won't be there to help,
Not there to save me from this void.
Not from a place like this,
But I still want you here.

Save this garden, give it life.
Give it something to live for.
Be someone's light.

Save me.

Can You Stand The Rain?

Kaitlyn Williams

Can you stand the rain?
That's my favorite song by New Edition,
Because I know there's not a lot of people that can't.

I know there's a lot of people as
Soon as a relationship gets hard, they give up.
As soon as the storms come and
There's thunder and lightning, they would
Rather run in the rain.

Than go inside and get an umbrella.

I know there are people that only think
A relationship is going to be like a summer
Day at the beach.

They think nothing is going to happen.
But when it starts to rain,
They just stand there and get wet.

Mondays

Kaitlyn Williams

Mondays.
Nobody likes them,

Because you still have four days left
Until the weekend.
Then on Sunday, you have to get ready to
Start the cycle over again.

Mondays.
Nobody likes them,

Because you have to sit in traffic for an hour
For what should be a fifteen-minute drive,
And you still gotta drop your kids off,
Then you're thirty minutes late to work.

Nevaeh Chaplin

Mondays.
Nobody likes them,

Because you ate all your food
During the weekend and
Have to go shopping, but you forget
Your wallet at home and have to
Stay hungry another day.

Mondays.
Nobody likes them,

Because they just suck.

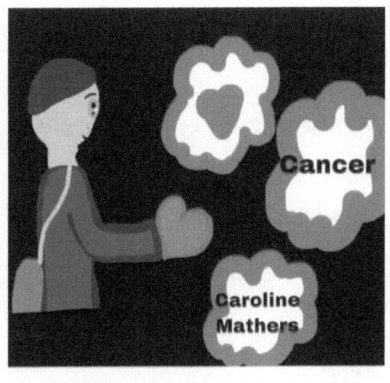

Nevaeh Chaplin

Court

Learric Green

Could there be a better way to handle things?
"You broke my tv. Give me 300$."
A tiny number of people will hand over
The money for the repairs and the others
Think they are a professional liar. Evidence
Is the carry to a win unless nobody has any,
Then it's just he said she said until
Something happens.

The Millionth Time

Ulises Oliva Tellez

He told me he loved me, but that's the millionth
Time I've heard that. I think he may be lying
Just because of how suspicious he looks.
All I can do is say I love you back, and I do

Mean that. This relationship isn't going well.
I may be calling him my EX by next week.
He told me he hated me, but that's the first
Time I've heard that from him. I think he's
Telling the truth now. Oh well, this is all just
Called on love and hate.

The Love I Give

Yudi Cano

I don't feel sorry for the way I love you
Because I know my love was pure.

I don't feel bad for the way I held you because
I know I felt like I was holding the whole entire world.

Even though your gone,
I don't feel bad for the way I loved you.

20 Lives

Monserrat Tinoco

20 Lives
That are all worth it.
They struggle but still try on it.
20 educations that will be important later on in life.
Yes they can act dumb but still want their work done.
Lots of headaches but you will see what you earn later.
20 sleepy heads.
20 people who act like they care.
20 kids can be so annoying.
They say teachers they hate school but still do the work.
They care but try to act cool.
20 kids who try to act so hard in front of people.

Three Little Words

Grace Ratliff

Hi.
How are you?

Three, three little words.
Nine letters, and rarely answered truthfully.

Good.
Do you really mean 'good'?
Or good enough that every ounce
Of your body isn't in pain?
Just most of it.
Good because you won't ask more questions if I say good.
Good because I should be happy.
Right?

Fine.
Are you really fine?
Or you don't want to bother anyone with your words
Because you don't want to trouble
Anyone more than they already are?
Fine because this is normal.
Hurting. Mentally. Physically.
It's normal.

I've gotten used to it. So I'm fine.

Those are lies
Most of everything is a lie
Let's be honest, shall we?

How are you?
I'm tired. I'm hurt.
I'm frustrated. I'm disappointed.
I'm confused.

Get sleep.
What'd you do?
Talk it out.
What happened?
Ask questions.

No.

I'm tired of hurting.
Hurting because I'm frustrated.
Frustrated because I'm disappointed in myself.
Disappointed because I'm confused.

Why am I confused?

How are you?
I'm doing good.

Cool

Nathaniel Irvin

Cool?

Your cool.

My cool.

No, your cool.

Micheal?

No, you're cool.

Our cool.

For goodness's sake, no.

You're cool.

Our're cool.

Wait, what?

Maggots Michael, you're eating maggots.

Maggots Michael, your eating maggots.

Not mine, thair yours and

I don't want your maggots.

Especially eating maggots.

Thair.

There're.

Thair're.

Thor.

Thor're.

Aisle sea y'all sewn.

What the world needs now:

Is love Bert Baccarac style.

Media Dance

Erik Hilden

Door slamming like classrooms closed,
Feet shuffling across black carpet stained
With sunflower seeds and gum and skittles and demons,
And the clock is ticking down to the end.

Cool crisp air like the lies they tell us about
Holiday cheer and snow falling on the horizon
We never see. Except in commercials.
The internet never lies.

And the fighting and violence and death and destruction
Will wear a Santa hat and "Ho Ho Ho!" its way
Into our living rooms to tell us that on that day
The clock ticked time down to its last.

And it was just okay.

Angela Gomez

9 Happy Endings?

Someone Ghot

Avaree Courtney

In a city, in a town, a big one, three friends, no older than 16, walked down a worn-down sidewalk. A sidewalk that had seen mythical beasts ten times bigger than the tallest point in the gloomy city. The streets had seen a time when the beasts had frolicked with the tiniest animal in this world. These creatures are what you hear about in the most absurd of cases. Though the creatures were indeed dangerous. Killing off half of the population in a matter of days the streets erupted in outrage demanding safety. But how every story goes the cases went cold and the creatures continued to live their lives with nothing more than a stern talking to.

"They're back at it again," A boy with a light brown complexion said.

"Who is Matteo?" A boy, taller than the first, with a much darker complexion, asked.

"Those creatures. The ones that are said to protect us," Matteo said.

He continued, "They've already accidentally killed a kid with a rouge bullet." Sarcasm and anger laced his voice.

"So nothing happened with the previous case, huh?" The taller boy asked.

"Nothing! I tell you, Joshuah, it's insane how much they get away with but when we do as much as jaywalk we are immediately told off, not to mention the slurs we get and being told where to go," Matteo spat.

"Okay, dude, first of all, you need to calm down, you look like a steamed vegetable. Second of all, Hazel did you hear anything in the news because of that?" Joshua asked.

"I wasn't up that early this morning. Sorry," A girl with fair skin, blue eyes, and wavy brown hair said.

"You're really lucky. You know that, right Hazel?" Matteo says with a sneer visible in his voice.

"How am I lucky?" Hazel said, confused.

"You don't have to fear those creatures coming for you. You can live happily ever after while Matteo and I have a big target on our backs." Joshua stated.

"He's right Hazel. You may be growing up in this world with us but you can go to sleep not worrying about one of those creatures showing up at your door to tell you that you get a one-way ticket back to "where you belong." Matteo said, annoyance visible in his tone.

Hazel looked into Joshua's tired eyes. His bags are visible from all of the all-nighters he has pulled to have a chance at surviving his Math class. His teachers think that he only has their class and not five others. Joshua had been complaining about all of the work.

Hazel stopped talking. In reality, she remembers that these guys she's known since the end of the fifth grade could end up dead in front of her never to see the warlocks or witches they call parents that neither of them ultimately liked to deal with but they loved them. Hazel thought she really knew what they went through but maybe she didn't.

"I want to understand but it's a little hard when I am always so confused about what you guys talk about. Both of you are so vocal and you work so hard. Why?" Hazel questions. She wanted to get to know these boys more than she already did.

Joshua paused and thought of the best way to word this.

"When a kid that looks like me fails school, another Jail Cell is built. We work hard so we can stay out of there. Whereas with you, well, you guys can just buy yourselves into an amazing school. You won't pay the price but the parents do and that's just fine. But if someone like a famous warlock did that and they looked like me, that's an entirely different story," Joshua said looking down.

"I want to know more about what happens in your neighborhoods," Hazel said. She knew this could go two ways. Either they wold tell it to her straight about what happens in the neighborhoods or she gets told off. Was this a good question to ask these boys? Her parents always told her that they were bad news but she always brushed it off.

"You want to know what happens?" Matteo asked,

surprised by the suddenness of the question.

"Yes," Hazel said with uncertainty in her voice. An eternal battle of what she could hear could be terrifying or perfectly normal like stuff that happens in her neighborhood.

"The creatures come to our neighborhoods every night." Joshua blurted out. Hazel just figured out why she barely saw the creatures in her neighborhood. They went to her friends to what? Torture them. Scare them? All she knows is that her friends have seen what might kill them years before they even go to the other side.

"What?" Hazel's voice was shaking. Her eyes showed clear distress.

"We haven't slept peacefully since the murder of a forty-five-year-old man simply because he stole a loaf of bread, It's scary Hazel," Matteo said with fear visible in his eyes. Maybe Matteo and Joshua weren't up all night due to studying but do tho the fear they may lose their lives or their families. Just that thought alone made Hazel want to throw up.

"Is...Is that why you guys look like you haven't been getting sleep? Or why when the schools' creature walks near you tense up? Is that why you guys look like you could pass out at any moment during English?" Hazel was worried about her friends. She was oblivious to what they were going through; she couldn't comprehend having to live in that type of fear 24/7. It sounded like a living nightmare. No. It WAS a living nightmare. A nightmare that may never end. A nightmare for some was a dream to others. Others that didn't want people like Matteo or Joshua here.

"And when we do end up sleeping on the way home in the subway, we're always on edge. There may not be a day when we're not. A day may come where we can sleep in peace but I doubt it." Joshua says letting out a yawn in the process.

The trio had been walking for one of the longest times. If you looked around from where they started in Hazel's neighborhood to the middle of the city standing in front of the highest point in their city.

Hazel turned around to see the few people that lined the streets. The humidity had subsided and the entire world seemed to slow down when she looked up all she could see was the colorful leaves that blew from the park at the very center of this monopolized city. A city that was driven on fake news, sympathy that meant nothing, "accidental" deaths that terrorized community after community, communities that wondered if they should just homeschool their kids.

She glanced at Joshua, who had put his dark green hoodie on.

"You like that hoodie, huh?" Matteo said, looking a little less feared and calmer.

"I mean Hazel got it for me, I think I'm required to wear it!" Joshua said shoving Hazel playfully.

Matteo pointed over to a small bookstore and suggested they go in.

The store was small and quaint but felt welcoming. The trio walked through the door and Matteo booked it for the dystopian section. Ever since Hazel had shown him "The Giver" he's never been the same. He did always say that he'd love to live in worlds like this. An ideal world. But a world that did not exist. A world that maybe even the author wanted but could only portray in detailed paragraphs. A world that one could only imagine.

Hazel stayed with Joshua because she didn't want to deal with the existential crisis Matteo was about to face. When the three finally rejoined together, which was an hour later because Matteo got caught up with some girl talking about K-Pop, they walked to the counter, Matteo was the only one to find something that sparked interest in him and whatever goes on in his mind.

Joshua's phone buzzed. Something from the news. A title that made his blood boil.

"Creatures Kill Innocent Unarmed Man." The picture of this man seemed familiar.
Joshua stormed out of the small shop. The sun was setting on this day readying for the next.

"Joshua, what's the matter?" Hazel said worried that this may end in one of the worst ways possible.

"Nothing is ever fair! It's all about the color of our skin! Armed or not! Never about what we're like," Joshua scrambled tears brimming his eyes. He didn't want to live in this kind of world. Sometimes he wanted to dig himself into his work and not worry about what was around him.

"Joshua look at me, and listen," Matteo said

"We both know we have targets on our backs, you need to calm down." Matteo continued trying to get his friend to breathe.

"NO! IT'S ALL ABOUT OUR SKIN COLOR! NEVER ABOUT ANYTHING ELSE ONLY OUR SKIN! GET THAT IN YOUR MIND! IT DOESN'T MATTER AT THIS POINT!" Joshua screamed at the top of his lungs. Hot tears ran down his face, his vision became blurry and his voice was cracking.

"JOSHUA, I DON'T WANNA LOSE YOU TO THEM! WE NEED YOU!" Matteo yelled back hearing his voice gets choked in his retaliation.

"Joshua, calm down," Hazel was going to continue but Joshua beat her to it.

"NO, I WON'T HAZEL! YOU DON'T HAVE TO LIVE YOUR LIFE IN FEAR! I DO! YOU GET TO LIVE YOUR HAPPILY EVER AFTER! I MAY NOT! I MAY DIE AT THE HANDS OF SOMEONE ELSE!" Joshua screeched doubling over. Sweat dripping from his face, spit had flown from his mouth. He was mad and he was barely holding himself together.

Matteo's eyes went wide when he looked behind Joshua.

They had heard Joshuas' screams of retaliation and they were mad.

They were huge standing six feet tall, muscles peeking from every corner of their body, their eyes darker than a midnight sky. They asked if anything was wrong and Joshua lost his cool.

He turned and punched one square in the jaw. But the creature didn't stumble. All it did was crack its humongous knuckles and both Matteo and Joshua were frozen in fear. Unable to move. Immobile.

The creatures grabbed and restrained Matteo and Hazel. Their fingers dug into their shoulders.

A creature from the back walked forward and put its dagger-like finger to Joshua's cheek.
Slice.

The dark liquid ran from the wound and it stung. Bad. But Joshua still wasn't finished. He was angry. Angry that his family has to fear for their lives, angry that all of those cases went cold, angry that he might not have a future. Right. He may not have a future. If he has to die at the hands of a creature as disgusting as this one, he was gonna fight.

His vision was blurred but he threw punches, he wanted them to feel all of the pain he felt every time he watched the news and he had to say goodbye to a classmate or the kid from down the street. All because no one would call attention to the intentional murder of his friends and family.

He was tired. Maybe he'd finally get a good night's rest for once. Maybe he wouldn't have to finish that research project he didn't start, maybe it was for the better. What if his death was the last straw for everyone. What if his death reopens every case that went cold. What if he could be the boil-over. The point where everything gets resolved. The point where they finally realize that everyone was human. Even those wretched creatures that were meant to protect them.

But maybe that wouldn't happen. Maybe everything stays the same.

And then it happened. Pain. Pain that felt like someone had crunched his insides. Maybe someone or something did.

Joshua looked up ignoring the screams of his friends. He looked up. The stars were so pretty. Maybe he could finally touch one.

Impact.

Impact onto the cold sidewalk. His body went into

a fetal position. He felt Hazel's hands on him as she tried to call for help. He looked at Matteo who was holding his hands at the wound site. Trying to control his tears. Joshua looked to his left. A beautiful city that had been corrupted and manipulated. One that had been divided by skin color. But if this was a tipping point, a lot was about to change.

Losing. He felt himself drifting. Lightheaded. Spotted vision. Losing his senses.
Hazel was losing it. She was hysterical and it was not any better for Matteo.

"I'm so sorry, please don't leave there still is so much stuff we haven't done...We still have to go to adopt that tiger you always wanted. Or get your star named after you. You have to go and visit the International Space Station. Joshua, don't leave us..." Hazel whispered, choking on her tears.

"Please...don't leave us… you have to stay awake Joshua....just stay awake…" Matteo said, his voice breaking.

"I love you guys…" Joshua said, before getting to finally touch the stars.

Mebron Cayabyab

The Fight For The Kingdom

Angle Perez

Once upon a time, there was a kingdom. It was happy, beautiful, and perfect. In the kingdom, there was a castle, and in the castle there lived a king. He wore a golden crown on top of his blond hair and a beautiful red velvet coat. The king loved his people, and the people loved the king. The king also had a wife and two sons that he loved very much. They were the perfect family. The king always took care of his people, and he never let them down. Any problem that came his way, he would always resolve. The king was not the king for the riches but because he cared for people. Everyone had homes to go back to and jobs to make money off. Everyone had food and water. The people paid taxes that were reasonable to their income. The cobblestone streets were always clean and the wood and cobblestone houses were always clean and organized. The entire kingdom was perfect.

There also lived a beast who was banished from the kingdom due to his past behavior. The beast had grey fur and sharp teeth that could easily cut through flesh and meat. The beast was very violent and always sought revenge. The beast had many talents, though. He was a skilled fighter, a master detective, and very astute. Although he was banished from the kingdom, he would still be hired by the king for some detective cases that the average detective in the kingdom could not do, but one day the beast started thinking, and then he made a plan to seek revenge for being banished from the kingdom by the king. His master plan was to spread a rumor that someone was planning to kidnap the king, he would get hired by the king and would get easy access to the castle where he could kidnap the king and declare himself as the new king.

As the beast expected, the king hired him to find the person planning to kidnap him. The beast then had to pretend he was trying to do the job. He went around the kingdom trying to find people that looked suspicious and he eventually found three people. He interrogated them one by one, asking the same set of questions. They all answered the questions while the beast stared straight into their eyes, but only one acted suspiciously and nervously. This suspect looked like he was hiding something, so the beast made him take the blame for planning to kidnap the king. The beast told the king that he had found the person who was planning to kidnap the king. The next day they both went to the suspect's house, but then the beast attacked. He knocked the king and the suspect out. He hid them in a secret house outside the kingdom. When the suspect woke up, the beast told him to move out of the kingdom and never come back and the suspect, out of fear, agreed. The beast told the people of the kingdom that because of the king's disappearance, he had been instructed to rule the kingdom.

The beast ruled the kingdom for two years. People were dying, going hungry, and were being treated poorly. There was violence all over the kingdom, and people hated the beast. People then started rioting and caused problems and chaos, but the beast did not care since there was nothing the people could do. The beast would visit the king and give him food and water to keep him alive, but then he decided to bring him to the caste and put him in a secret room that only the king and beast knew about. The room was not as bad as a prison cell. It was more of a royal cell. It had a full-size bed with carpet, lights, and books that the king could read if he wanted to. It was not that bad, but sometimes the beast would take the king to the balcony of the castle that overlooked the kingdom while no one was looking. The king would watch and see his kingdom and people fall apart while the king could do nothing about it besides hope for the best for his kingdom and people.

One day when the king was reading a book while he was at the lowest point of his life. He heard a voice, he looked and saw a gold glowing creature.

"Hey, I'm here to help you."

"Who's that?" asked the king.

"I'm a fairy, and I am here to help you get out of here."

"I thought fairies were myths," said the king.

"Well, we're not, and before I help you, you must promise that you will not tell anyone about me or else a curse will come upon you, a curse worse than death," said the fairy.

"I promise to not mention you, but how am I going to get out of here?" asked the king.

"Well, do you know anyone that can get you out?" asked the fairy

The king started thinking and said, "Hmm, actually, I do. A ninja, he is the best of the best. No one knows who he is, but I know he lives in the kingdom."

The fairy disappeared and went on the mission to find the ninja. The fairy went back to the village that it came from and got a book that has the name and location of everyone that lives in the kingdom. Eventually, the fairy found the ninja and the fairy told the ninja everything. The ninja agreed to help, but he was going to need time to plan. The fairy agreed and, eventually, the ninja came up with a plan and was ready to execute it. The ninja went through a creepy forest to the castle. When he got there, he went through the back entrance and snuck his way until he got to the king's room. He then proceeded to find a lever that opened a bookcase, which led to the secret room the king was being kept.

"Thank you for helping me, brother," said the king.

"Yes, your welcome, but we have to go right now before guards show up and run into some trouble," said the ninja.

They went to the ninja's house, where they organized a plan to defeat the beast. They planned to gather the five warriors, enter the castle, and fight till the end.

They gathered the warriors, and they all got to the castle. They fought their way through the bodyguards and got to the main room where the beast was waiting for them, unsurprised. They had a huge fight. Swords were being swung everywhere you could hear the sound of metal being hit against metal. The beast was ruthless and showed no mercy. Two warriors got knocked out, one was injured, and only the king, ninja, and one warrior were left. They fought till the end, and the beast was finally defeated. Then the king proceeded to ask him where his family was.

"Where is my family?" asked the king.

"Why would you think I would tell you. What will I get in return if I tell you?" said the beast.

"I will consider letting you go," the king said hesitantly.

"And why should I believe you?" asked the beast.

"Because I am the king, after all."

"Fine, but first, let me go, and then I will tell you," said the beast.

"You're crazy if you think I trust you after what you have done. Tell me now, or I will leave your fate in the hands of the people, and I think that you don't want that," said the king angrily.

"Fine, when I became king, I knew they were going to be a problem, so I sent them to a house not too far from here and told them if they ever came back, I would lock them up," explained the beast.

"Thanks, guards take him away," said the king.

"What! You said you would let me free," said the beast.

"I said I would consider letting you free," said the king.

The king found his family, and they were happy to see each other. They went back to the castle and the king fixed everything in the kingdom and they lived happily ever after.

Angela Gomez

Addis Coronel

The Impatient Protest

Bennett Coronel

Once upon a time, in a nation, lived elves, two types of elves. Both of them being a different race of elves. The light-skinned elves being the most respected, the ones with the most rights. Being undisturbed by most of the people in the Elf Nation. The ones with an easy life set by their ancestors. Then you have the dark-skinned elves, the ones who don't have it as easy as the light-skinned elves.

Some being killed, injured, or falsely accused of something they didn't do. Of course, not all of them are bad elves. It's just the image that the light-skinned elves have on them; the bad image. Their past and recent history are what have caused them to form this image, otherwise, they would be living a life like the light-skinned elves.

None of the light-skinned elves could understand what the dark-skinned elves were going through. The killing, framing, and arrests on their color and family. Losing family members happened everywhere. They could've been killed by their kind arrested. Getting killed mostly happened from their kind. The bad image that they made others believe. The other times they get killed or arrested happen by the hands of the light-skinned elves.

Only some light-skinned elves did this. However, only some were discriminating against the dark-skinned elves. These were the ones getting them arrested. The police. The light-skinned police, but not all of them. The ones who hated them for no apparent reason. Just the bad image of them was what drove them to get all of them arrested. Either pulling them over on the road or comparing them to a description that doesn't match up with them at all. They could've been put in handcuffs and on their way to jail for a crime they didn't commit. Either that or they get shot. Shot for reaching for a weapon. A weapon that doesn't even exist. Many were aware of these events, however. The witnesses that record these incidents. The ones who publish these videos online for others to see.

Most of the time these would lead to evidence for getting them out of jail. Or this would cause some serious trouble for the cop that caused this to happen in the first place. If there wasn't a punishment for the cop then elves that were light and dark would make a mini protest which would get the cop what they deserve for their irresponsible actions.

Many dark-skinned elves were able to relate to

these things. Sarah, a college student, in a city, has seen and heard many things throughout her life. She was one of those people that could relate to these types of situations. Her brother was falsely accused of assaulting another girl. Her father were almost killed by a light-skinned cop for reaching for a weapon in his vehicle. And finally, her uncle, killed for "resisting" arrest. Many things have happened to her family, but nothing has really happened to her. Nothing that would bring concern to others. But no one will be left alone forever. Sarah began to recall those memories.

"The most unforgettable moment I will ever have in my life," said Sarah when being interviewed. One day, which seemed like an ordinary day, was when it happened. Sarah and her cousin, April, were going shopping in the city.

"So what are you going to get April?" said Sarah.

"I was thinking of getting a new outfit for the party next weekend. And you? What are you interested in buy-ing?" replied April.

"I think a new outfit and those new designer shoes."

"Wait what's that?"

"What are you talking about?"

"Is someone saying they can't breathe?"

"Now that you mention I can hear it. I think it's just in front of this car."

Both turned the corner as horror filled their eyes. When most things go wrong for dark-skinned elves, it tends to happen in uncommon places. Places where rarely any people passed by. The arrest or murder of a dark skin elf for no reason. Horror filled their eyes, seeing something so tragic and horrific in broad daylight. In the city, near a parked car on the side of a road, was a light-skinned cop with his knee on a dark-skinned elf. Both of them could tell what was wrong with this. That "restraint" that the cop was doing wasn't going to restrain him but kill him. Sarah immediately pulled out her phone and started recording.

April noticed that there wasn't just one cop, but there were three more behind the car.

Then the man that was in this "restraint" said,"Please stop, I can't breathe!"

After a minute or so, more people started to take notice of what was happening. Dark and light-skinned elves were watching this event take place. Some decided to record as well. Gasping for carbon dioxide, the man is still saying," I can't breathe." Sarah, April, and the other witnesses were yelling at the cop, with his knee on his neck, to stop. All of them were able to visually tell that he couldn't breathe. The cop didn't listen and kept his knee on his neck. Time went on for five minutes, then ten minutes, and finally, fifteen minutes where everyone was scared to their inner core. He wasn't responding anymore.

No response. The four cops had realized that he wasn't waking up and tried to wake him up. Soon they called an ambulance. They loaded him onto the ambulance which was where all the witnesses last saw him. He was later pronounced dead. Sarah and April left their shopping and went home in shock. Once they got home was when they realized that he was dead. Sarah had the full video and others recorded the unfortunate event as well. She uploaded it and so did the other witnesses.

"I had to upload this event. It's not something I have to quiet about," said Sarah when being interviewed.

Sarah's video showed the full story while the others showed different angles and different viewpoints. It spread like a wildfire. Millions of elves saw the event and it was on the news everywhere in the nation. The next day was peaceful, but the last one they were going to have in a while.

Protests took place. The HPD (Helvert Police Department) was the police station with the four cops enlisted. Protesters were telling the HPD to fix the matter at hand. They weren't going to let something like this occur and not do something about it. The corruption and the abuse of power of the police were very apparent in that single video. How the police are just able to kill anyone with no one getting in their way. Not only was it just the HPD, but multiple police departments were getting protested against across the nation. Elves across the nation realized that some of their police departments weren't what it seemed to be so they began to protest. The HPD and other police departments across the nation were trying to figure out what way they were going to address the matter and fix it.

Days went by and no response from the HPD. The protesters began to get impatient. They were seriously wondering if they even cared about what happened. Anger and hate started to build up inside of the protesters. The elves were now getting furious. They had the idea to take matters into their own hands and did the exact opposite of a protest.

A riot. Riots were the only way that they were going to get the police to listen to them. The exact opposite of a protest. A protest is meant to be peaceful and get a point across. A riot is when all hell breaks loose. They started to burn buildings with their fire crystals. Fire crystals will make a mini fireball when crushed in one's hand. The bigger the crystal, the bigger the fireball. They are mined, sold to shopkeepers, and are then sold to the people. Many people would launch the miniature, blazing, and fiery sphere onto buildings and statues to burn them down. They slowly start to collapse with all of the burning rubble falling to the ground and turning into dust and smaller pieces at the point of impact.

The windows of the shops were getting shattered by rocks thrown by the rioters. The glass would crack open and all of the shards of glass would fall to the concrete floor, shining from the light reflecting off of it, and shattering into miniature pieces once hitting the floor. The HPD and other police departments had to stop with their plan as these riots were starting to get out of control. They sent out police who started to throw elf repellent at the rioters.

Every single one of the elves backed up as no elve would ever love a foul smell. Baby diapers, smelly armpits, and the smell of sewers was something no elf wanted to smell like. Yet there were some with protective magic that protected them from the smell and this caused them to throw the elf repellent back at the police.

Fires were still visible the next day and more things started to happen. Looting took place. The rioters had started to break into local stores and steal anything that was valuable or something that would cost some cash. This would later bite them back.

The police tried many attempts to stop the rioters in their tracks, but they didn't care about a thing they said. In return, they started to say,"You guys hate dark-skinned elves." They called them corrupt and they wanted justice for the man killed on that day. Looting started from local stores to even more expensive stores. They would break in and start to steal whatever was worth of value. This wasn't the only new thing that they were doing. Vandalism started to take place. They would spray permanent dust onto the walls of buildings. They would make this permanent dust by getting special herbs and plants. Afterwards they would grind it into dust which caused it to turn into permanent dust. They wrote," DARK SKINNED ELVES MATTER!" They would also write on the walls very unappealing and rude things about the police.

This turned into an ongoing cycle that would just keep repeating itself every day. Riots, fires, looting, and vandalism. They forgot what the reason was and why they were doing this. A few months later the HPD decided that it would be a good thing to disestablish itself and to reconstruct itself alongside its people. Other places across the nation were able to fix their corruption without having to disestablish themselves.

Yet it still wasn't an easy feat for them to accomplish.

Then there were other places. The places that knew how to do a protest. The place that could wait for an answer as long as it was getting fixed. The place where they could trust each other. These people believed that their police department was going to be able to resolve the problem and to fix any corruption. The place where there isn't really any sign of discrimination. The place that knew what peaceful meant.

The rioters were now happy and had joy for a brief moment. Just a moment before they had to look back. To look back at all of the things they did to get their "point" across. To look back at all of the destruction they had caused. They used a man's death as an excuse for chaos without even realizing it.

Angela Gomez

Olivia Summerlin

A Broken World

Olivia Summerlin

Sometime and somewhere in the history of the universe, it seems as if the life of one planet was about to end. On a Mars-like, planet there is a worldwide "infection" that has been broadcasted throughout the world. Some people can recover from the infection but others fall victim to the terrible fate that had patiently awaited them. One girl in particular named Anna and her trusty friend Suru, a cat who would follow Anna to the end of the world, was part of this epidemic. It's almost funny to look upon a couple of lives because when compared to the whole world, don't their lives almost seem trivial?

The people who had gotten infected would turn into zombie-like creatures who could easily spread the illness. The government issued and warned people to only go outside for necessities and when you did you would have to wear protective gear. You were also not allowed to be with friends or family for they could easily catch the illness. Many people feared the new illness spreading around so they listened to the government and took heed of their words. The illness had no limits as to who it would consume. You could be of cat species, dog species, or you could be a human. The illness didn't care and lacked any sense of remorse.

When Anna would go out in her gear and protection, it almost appeared as if the planet had been abandoned. She could walk miles down her road and not see a single soul that would indicate life.

This was probably because everyone was scared and listening to the government. Of course, you would see the occasional person out. Some people didn't even wear protective gear which made people think they were crazy.

It gave people thoughts such as "Do they want to die?" But there was nothing much the government could do since it was illegal for the government to control the entirety of a person's actions. So, the government just made protective gear a requirement when you entered a store or place where many people might linger. The protective gear was a type of bodysuit that covered every inch of your body. It looked strangely similar to a suit an astronaut would wear.

One by one, more and more people began to lose their jobs which caused lower-income and greatly affected her country's economy. People were fighting and burning down businesses and other structures in the already hard times in the name of justice. A person of the cat species, like Suru, was wrongly killed by a government official. Everyone felt bad for that cat as well as other cats but burning down struggling businesses, looting them, and breaking their windows weren't gonna do anything about the issue that government officials had with cats. Anna just wanted everything to be normal again. This might have been the lowest point of her planet in all of its history.

In Anna's and Suru's world, unlike on Earth, animals have human intelligence and are an avid part of their world's society. There are all different types of animals but some are said to have more power than others. This being said, everyone in their society is supposed to be equal so the idea of having some people think that people are equal and others not, is quite ironic. Yes, humans are part of this society, but they are not the only species in this world. In this world, animals have just as much a right to a fulfilling life as a human or any other species of animal that might oppose them. Even though there was a bit of a bumpy relationship between the cat species and humans, Anna and Suru were one of the many friends that were a pair of both humans and cat.

Sometimes, Suru and Maiya would communicate through old broken walkie-talkies, staring out at the sky as if to find an answer to their world's problems. She missed the beautiful orange and velvet-colored sky that held up two moons of a distant planet. She missed the short almost wheat-colored grass being trimmed by yard workers. The smell of fresh orange-ish dirt that came directly from the dry earth she called her home. All of that seemed dull now. All of the beauties of her world were seeming to fade away. Like tears in the rain. There was a cliff that Suru and Anna visited before the mass illness had begun. The friends would look out over the horizons at her world's beauty. Anna started to remember a conversation that she and Suru had and it went a little like this.

"Suru" Anna called out while looking out over the horizon.

"What is it, Anna?" Suru asked curiously.

"Do you think we'll always be together? Will we always be close friends?" asked Anna in a saddening tone.

"Yes, I do. Lookout at the horizon. Do you see the water reflecting the sunlight? Do you see how the sun is kindly caressing the sun?" Suru said while extending his index finger forward.

"Yes?" Anna said, confused.

"I think we will always stay together. Like how the water is caressing the sun, we will caress each other will we not?" said Suru.

Thinking back to this moment almost made Anna want to cry. She wanted to set things straight. She knew she needed to do something about the illness fast. That night Anna thought silently in her empty house while looking out of the window. She came to no conclusions. She didn't know what to do. She eventually fell asleep succumbing to the dark night skies that crossed her open window. Suru, being a long way away, stayed up the whole night feeling a sense of loss. Was it because he couldn't see Anna? Was it because of the unjust killings of the cat species? He didn't know and he, like Anna, wouldn't come to an answer either.

A couple of nights passed and Anna, as well as Suru, still found no answers in the night sky. They couldn't, for the answer lied within the night. When the sun was being held up, shining brightly in the afternoon sky. The next day Anna was talking on her broken walkie-talkie to Suru when she froze. Off in the distance, she saw something.

"A gathering?" She thought.

Why would there be a gathering during the illness? This struck Anna's curiosity. She quickly told Suru she had to go and put down the walkie-talkie. Suru continued to talk asking why she had to go be the only answer he got was silence. Anna had already slipped into her astronaut-like protective gear and was heading towards the gathering.

Her pace began to pick up and started to turn into a run. She ran and she didn't look back. She had bright starlit eyes which only grew wider as she got closer to the gathering. For the first time since the illness she saw people smiling even if it was through their gear, they were still smiling. She saw that in the people's hands were ropes. Moderately long ones. Instead of holding hands, for safety, they held ropes.

One person holding one end and the next holding the other end. It was quite the spectacle. When she finally started making it towards the gathering her pace began to slow. Every type of person was joining together. Christians, atheists, dogs, cats, birds, humans, everyone. Every type of person and creature resided together with their suits on.

They were standing in a large circular shape around the old magic crystal which her town used and dried up long ago. Magic in today's society was dead and practically non-existent. Even so, the magic crystal still played a big part in symbolizing her country and representing her country's history. Seeing the sight of everyone come together was quite beautiful indeed. It made Anna start to hope and dream. The beautiful sight of these people gave Anna a passing thought. To get through these hard times everyone needed to come together.

"Staying independent and only worrying about our-selves isn't gonna get us anywhere. We need to work and come together even if it isn't in person" Anna thought. Her eyes grew wide as she had surprised herself with such a trivial explanation to the new everyday horrors. With a slight smirk on her face, she lightly brushed off the idea for it was simply that.

An idea. A passing thought.

Without saying a word Anna found an empty side of a rope and grabbed on. In the middle of this diverse group of people, she stood holding one side of a rope that was connecting her to everybody. She wondered why she was holding on so tight but finally came to the conclusion that she just wanted everything to be back to normal. Like how life was before the illness.

Maybe, in Anna's mind, the rope represented a bridge back to her own world. The world she used to know.

Slowly her society, if not her world, began to recover and was eventually able to stand up again. Life was not com-pletely the same but nothing is after disasters. Seeing happy people, crisp orange skies, and a wonderful work-ing society almost brought tears to Anna's eyes. She was happy that the illness was over and that others could share the same joy she was feeling at that moment. Her world was able to come back because of the people who came together despite their differences. Anna and Suru were finally able to return to their long path of a happily ever after once again.

Angela Gomez

10 A Sonnet In Your Bonnet

About Me

Mia Trejo

My name is Mia and I like to eat.
I do not have a favorite cookie.
All I do is sleep, eat, game, and repeat.
I play genshin but I am a rookie.

I do not have a favorite color.
If I had to pick though it would be red.
I'm a good kid so I have no lover.
I like fictional characters instead.

My favorite people are my best friends.
KaLeah, Sydney, Bennett, Iyana.
My siblings are nice it just depends.
My two sisters are Amy and Ana.

My favorite anime character.
Yelena I'll do anything for her.

Love Can Be An Absolute Pain

Hailee Gudrunardottir

Love can be an absolute pain, really.
It can heal your heart or it can kill it.
Love can be given every day freely,
Like a warmth that your heart needs to heal it.

People have had their fair share of loving.
It is not something they can learn fast.
Some people just think it isn't their thing,
But maybe it has to do with their past.

Love can hurt like it is the end of life,
But it can be a beautiful thing too.
Love can stab you in the heart like a knife,
But that does not mean you should feel so blue.

Love can be inside all over me.
So how hard can it really, truly be?

Days Of The Week

Maria Garcia

Today is Monday and I feel alone.
Watching the moon makes me feel so much worse.
I hope I will soon be out of this zone,
When will be the end of this stressful curse.

It is now Wednesday and I feel better.
Seeing my best friend brought my feelings up.
With lots of things in my mind, I upset her.
I felt bad so I brought her a cute cup.

Friday is next and I feel excited.
Could not be any happier for this.
My best friend told me something unexpected.
She is going to be having a sis.

People go through different emotions,
And can be the reason for some actions.

Olivia Summerlin

Sweet Science Of Boxing

Jack Garcia Linarte

Thou filled with anger swinging for the fence.
Warriors who are considered as brave,
With no guidance become animals hence,
A trainer who tells them how to behave.

T'is we seperate the men from the boys
Those with heart and perseverance succeed.
While others break as easily as toys,
Thou drops many tears, as man is seen bleed.

Men fight for their legacy and their pride
As thou pride gone in a blink of an eye.
Weaving not to tie, they move like their flies,
Where the loser is left only to cry.

Some fight feeling they have something to prove.
While others seek glory to feel approved.

School

Marlene Gonzalez

Another school day is yet to arrive.
I always dread for these days to appear.
However for good grades I go and strive.
That is why I keep trying every year.

The good part is that I get to see friends.
They are the fun part of a long school day.
It is a joy to see as the day ends.
The time flies as it is already May.

New teachers, new classrooms are waiting.
That is the worst part of starting again.
New year, new people, friends are awaiting.
Go back, you say, to counting one through ten.

So young you once were but not any more.
The memories go flying out the door.

Revenge Consumes Betrayal

Teandra Johnson

I have been betrayed by one who lied through.
They understood me, yet left me alone.
I wouldn't dare touch dangerous taboo,
Except this time when you see their white bone.

The friendship we had, so strong and lovely,
But you messed it all up and I hate you!
There will be no time for recovery,
Blood will bleed and puddle like thickened stew.

The chances you had are now fully done!
You scream and you scream and you scream, shut up!
Don't even try to escape, just don't run.
Now you've tripped. Stop the yapping, you dumb pup.

I can end it all, like snipping a thread,
What can you possibly do with no head?

Your Tragic Demise

Emma Daley

Of your empty bed, filled with dust and dirt,
Shall I sit here and wait for your return?
Oh how you filled me with a twisting hurt,
I regret the days I left you to burn.

Without your presence, the walls speak too loud.
Dare you leave me in this cold, heartless place?
Your hatred of me you should have avowed.
I wanted nothing more than your embrace.

I wish to know if you are resting well,
As I pace this endless hallway of grief,
Tis' my time to wish you a big farewell
My heart is strained from hoping for relief.

I shall walk this doleful, bare earth alone,
As my sorrow is far too overgrown.

Fishies, So Many Fishies

Avaree Fludd

Fishies, fishies, oh, so many fishies.
There are so many of them, red and blue.
These fishies, oh, could be so pure squishy.
If I touched one, the things that would ensue.

Dear, it is a different world down here.
The fishies are not as cute as they seem.
If we touch those fishies we disappear.
The fishies don like it when we do scream

However, we know that they are lying.
Don't look back, they have lied to all of us.
But we know that no one is replying.
They have somehow silenced us, all at once.

So don't go thinking fishes are so clean
Because the fishes will let no one scream.

Oh Sonnets

Angel P. Guarneros

Oh sonnets, you seem oh so very hard.
Oh so very complicated indeed.
Oh, why so many rules you shall follow?
Oh sonnets, so very perfect sonnets.

But you know it's not as so very hard.
It's not so very hard as it may seem
When you know what to do when writing these,
It becomes easy like riding a bike.

Just know what you are doing and it's cake.
Just count your syllables as your numbers.
Just know your complicated sonnet rules,
And you shall succeed in writing sonnets.

Now it is time to climb and write sonnets.
Oh, this sonnet was fun and now I'm done.

The Exquisite Shale Rock

Nevaeh Chaplin

Shall I show thee the most exquisite shale?
The shale rock resembles layers of cake.
Some may be the vastness of a blue whale
The blue whale size shale maybe hard to break.

Mixed sediments compacted into one
Broken rocks creating mosaic art.
Pressured cementation with help from sun
If thee look, see the different rock parts.

Now that you want to see look at the rock
It looks exquisite like your almond eyes
It looked like a whale shaped big piece of chalk
Now you see I was not telling thee lies

Thee may have a different point of view,
But now thee see the descriptions are true.

President. Snow

Olivia Summerlin

Parents

Mia Trejo

Mexican bread is so good I love it.
My mom makes delicious food everyday.
I hate some foods and it's hard to admit,
With the food I hate I throw it away.

My parents don't like it when I waste food.
If I do waste food they get very mad.
When they get angry they ruin the mood,
Then I think it's my fault and I feel bad.

Even though they make me mad I love them.
I am thankful to have loving parents.
We don't talk as much but there is still chem.
I wish I could be very transparent.

I wish I was able to trust them more.
I wish things were like how they were before.

School

Maria Garcia

School can be hard sometimes and confusing.
Lunch is my favorite part of the day.
And then I see people outside running.
I sit outside with my friends and don't play.

During my first class, I get to relax.
But not for too long, just a few minutes.
While we wait, the teacher let us eat snacks.
In school, there can be several limits.

Every classroom has a different rule.
Some of them are strict, and others are not.
The teachers can be serious but cool.
But classrooms can be annoyingly hot.

School is about to end for everyone.
After that, we will not see anyone.

A Lover's Tale

Jack Garcia Linarte

With a contagious smile and lovely smell,
Nothing can stop me from thinking of you.
Thou body is wax, perfect you can tell.
Thou is perfect even the way you chew.

I wish she would be mine until the end.
I even learned how to handle the kids.
She will be mine. I can only pretend.
She has now shut down my dream with some lids.

She has found a new lover as I wait.
Wait, hoping she will have seen her mistake.
She may not know who I am, which I hate.
I hope my love for her is proven fake.

I hope it is fake so there is less pain.
Although she will have a place in my brain.

Him

Marlene Gonzalez

He is old, with the face of a young child.
He hasn't aged since he was six years old.
Back in the olden days, he always smiled.
But now he has turned grumpy and quite cold.

His face, round and soft, like a little kid.
His hair is light brown and his eyes dark brown.
He was always too shy so he just hid.
Now he is known and the talk of the town.

It is said he takes kids who are alone.
Many kids go missing they think it's him,
But he just wants to be in his own zone.
They think he's cruel because they say he's grim.

But really he is just another man.
He shouldn't be treated anything less than.

How The Sheep Cries

Teandra Johnson

On this very cold stormy winters night,
The sheep huddle together nice and warm.
Though one is awake and she sees with sight,
How the vicious creatures arrive and swarm.

Everyone awake, they're going to eat us!
Is what she screams to save her fellow sheep.
No matter how loud she screams and makes fuss,
They continue to snore and snooze, still sleep.

Oh how the creatures, silently they prowl,
The jagged fangs they wear to shred them half.
Her ears are filled with their deep and loud growl,
She must save the sheep and the cow's live calf!

This winter on the animal filled farm,
Now a feeding ground for the wolves to harm.

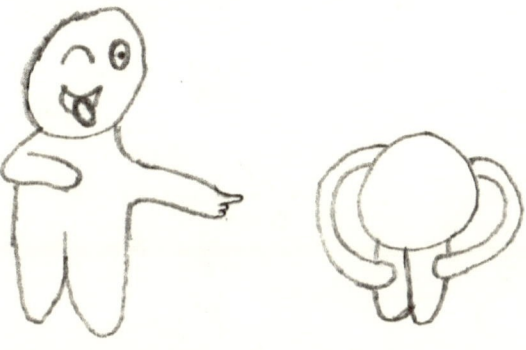

Ulises Oliva Tellez

Coming Of Age

Emma Daley

So much to learn, life full of innocence.
The stars, a nightlight for the lurking beasts.
An imagination full of nonsense.
A table full of sweets and treats, a feast.

A feeling of loss and mere confusion,
How I wish to shield your eyes of the ill.
It is nothing more than an illusion.
What lies beneath will give you quite the thrill.

Such beasts hide no longer, curtains aside.
A world of no light, a bottomless pit.
Venturing alone, a treacherous ride.
Many fall so early, you must not quit.

A moment of deserved peace and silence.
With your wise words, someone needs your guidance.

Well, It Seemed...

Angel P. Guarneros

Look at the oh so very dark blue sea.
The very bright sun shining overhead.
No clouds to be seen, no voices to hear.
What a nice day to sail through the ocean.

You can hear the waves crashing underneath.
You can feel the cold breeze hitting your face,
As the sun's light beams hit you with their heat.
Nothing could possibly go wrong today.

Oh wait, are those storm clouds in the blue sky?
Are big, dark storm clouds rolling towards me?
Now it's dark, cold, and colorless out here.
No sun to be seen, no one to be heard.

The beautiful blue sky withdrew away.
Perhaps I spoke and awoke the huge storm.

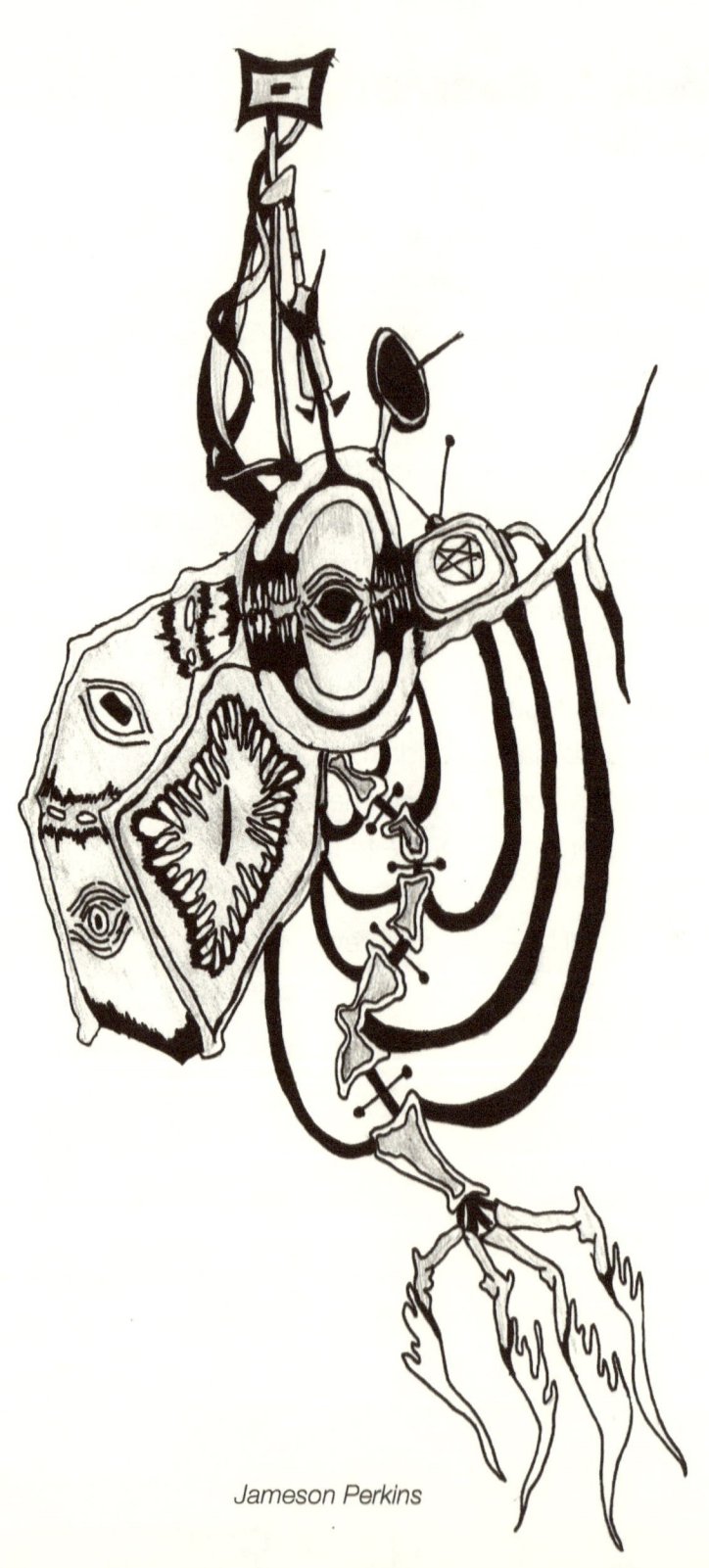

Jameson Perkins

11 By The Numbers

Seven

Angela Gonzalez Gomez

Seven players

Seven boys

Seven girls

Seven musicians

Seven cars

Seven assignments

Seven thoughts

Seven faces

Seven writers

Seven readers

Seven poetry

Seven essays

Better

Traquam Jones

Better year.
Better thoughts
Better grades.
Better leadership.
Better county.
Better laws.
Better future.
Better mind.
Better focal.
Better life.
Better friendship.
Better treatment.

Ahmyah Jackson

Five

Aldrey Lopez

Five basketball players
Five dreams
Five prayers
Five angrys emotions
Five thoughts
Five maybes
Five assignments
Five happy faces
Five emails
Five years
Five goals
Five nurses

Three

Christopher Sparks

Three curses
Three lives
Three homes
Three hearts
Three times
Three parts
Three letters
Three lovers
Three pushes
Three urges
Three passions

Faydrya Williams

Thirty

Antione Spillers

Thirty players
Thirty lives
Thirty athletes
Thirty prospects
Thirty helmets
Thirty hurdles
Thirty shoulder pads
Thirty families cheering
Thirty cars going from game to game
Thirty brothers
Thirty young men coming together
Thirty talent coming together as one

Different

Arrianna Walker

Different Thoughts
Different Personalities
Different Goals
Different Race
Different Clothes
Different Faces
Different Stories to tell
Different Future
Different Past
Different Dreams
Different Power
Different Beauty
Opposites that attract

Emma Daley

Twenty

Dayomi Banuelos

Twenty sleepy people.

Twenty hungry people.

Twenty lives.

Twenty soon to be freshmans.

Twenty school shirts.

Twenty chromebooks.

Twenty smiles.

Twenty tried people.

Twenty homework assignments due.

Twenty upcoming highschoolers.

Twenty pairs of shoes in a classroom.

Twenty students.

Mia Trejo

Many Numbers

Faydrya Williams

One teacher.
Fourteen students.
Two dreaming.
Six working hard.
Five off in space.
Three trying get by.
One hanging on tread.
Fourteen having problems.

A Room Full

Trawley Harper

A room full of students who have dreams
A room of students who have goals
A room of students who try their best
A room of students who want to do something with their
lives
A room of students who want to live life
A room of students who want to be teenagers
A room of students who want to have fun

Thirty-One

Ahmyah Jackson

Thirty-one futures,
Thirty-one dreamers,
Thirty-one believers,
Thirty-one achievers,
Thirty-one desires,
Thirty-one people to inspire,
Thirty-one teachers,
Thirty-one first responders,
Thirty-one lawyers,
Thirty-one nurses,
Thirty-one bakers,
Thirty-one goals,
Thirty-one thinkers,
Thirty-one motivators,
Thirty-one go-getters,

Alexis Bacani

Thirty-one money makers,

Thirty-one geniuses,

Thirty-one personalities,

Thirty-one soon to be billionaires,

Thirty-one soon to be millionaires,

Thirty-one destinies to manifest,

Thirty-one souls,

Thirty-one individuals full of integrity,

Thirty-one different walks of life,

Thirty-one dynasties,

Thirty-one doers,

Thirty-one tryers,

Thirty-one fighters,

Thirty-one different passions,

Thirty-one people who are dedicated,

Thirty-one individuals ready to transform the world.

Thirty More

Trawley Harper

30 different paths,
30 different futures,
30 different personalities,
30 learners,
30 high schoolers,
30 graduates,
30 eyeballs,
30 ideas,
30 new grenations,
30 different hard work.

Thirty

Jayden Snipe

Thirty students.
Thirty dreams.
Thirty hopes of fancy cars.
Thirty wishes of superpowers.
Thirty sleepy heads.
Thirty chairs filled up.
Thirty blank zoom screens.
Thirty kids talking.
Thirty thoughts of going home.
Thirty 8th graders going to high school...hopefully.

Twenty-Nine

Trawley Harper

Twenty-nine scholars
Twenty-nine historians
Twenty-nine songs
Twenty-nine paths
Twenty-nine goals
Twenty-nine dreams
Twenty-nine futures
Twenty-nine reasons
Twenty-nine hard workers
Twenty-nine successors
Twenty-nine personalities
Twenty-nine happy faces

Maria Garcia

Many Students

Lilliana Baker

Many students.
Many lives.
Many hard workers.
Many scholars.
Many believers.
Many minds.
Many hearts.
Many mathematicians.
Many scientists.
Many history makers.
Many pasts.
Many futures.

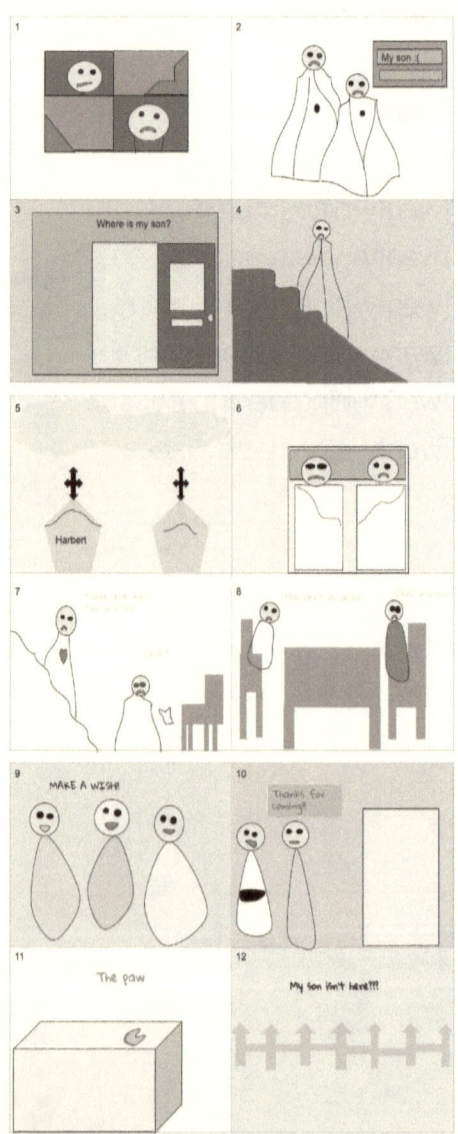

Aldrey Lopez

Twenty-Seven

Jave'yon Blake

Twenty-Seven dreams.

Twenty-Seven assignments done.

Twenty-Seven procrastinators.

Twenty-Seven scholars.

Twenty-Seven families.

Twenty-Seven answers.

Twenty-Seven Essays.

Twenty-Seven careers.

Twenty-Seven graduates.

Thirty-Two

Zyera Brown

Thirty-two honors students.

Thirty-two high expectations.

Thirty-two essays.

Thirty-two attitudes.

Thirty-two opinions.

Thirty-two tests.

Thirty-two mouths.

Thirty-two mouths.

Thirty-two "honors students"

Twenty-Seven

Nevaeh Chaplin

Twenty-seven entries

Twenty-seven names

Twenty-seven personalities.

Twenty-seven screens.

Twenty-seven ceilings.

Twenty-seven thinking about

What they are going to do next.

Twenty-seven poems to write.

Twenty-seven chapters to read.

Twenty-seven typing in the chat.

Twenty-seven questions.

Twenty-seven trying to finish their assignments on time.

Twenty-seven hoping to get an A.

Twenty-seven looking forward to Honors ELA 2.

Twenty-seven things that I am going to do?

Twenty-seven styles.

Twenty-seven goals.

Twenty-seven future graduates.

Twenty-seven hoping to get into a good school.

Twenty-seven acceptances.

Twenty-seven wanting to move on to the next step.

Twenty-seven happy faces.

Twenty-seven in the action of doing homework.

Twenty-seven emotions.

Twenty-seven ideas.

Twenty-seven wanting to pass.

Twenty-seven honors students.

Twenty-seven futures to think of.

Twenty

Bennett Coronel

Twenty minds.
Twenty pasts.
Twenty hopes.
Twenty lights.
Twenty educations.
Twenty futures.
Twenty masks.
Twenty unknowns.
Twenty truths.
Twenty lies.
Twenty illusions.
Twenty dreams.

Angel Perez Guarneros

Thirteen

Emma Daley

Thirteen hours.
Thirteen months.
Thirteen years.
Thirteen wishes.
Thirteen dreams
Thirteen books
Thirteen schools
Thirteen teachers
Thirteen sighs of relief.

Many Students

Jack Garcia Linarte

Many students
Many goals
Many plan for what's next
Many hope for the best
Many prayed to the lord, to be the very best
Many athletic
Many work hard
Many rise to the occasion
Many fall into the pit of dark with no way out
We have been prepared for the journey
Many hope to be something in this dark and scary world.

And We Hope

Avaree Fludd

In a world where we hope.
And we hope.
And maybe even hope some more.
In a world where we try our best
and we sometimes fail ourselves.
Therefore, we fail them.
The ones that always tried to push us.
We become disappointed.
When all we are is a number.
Sometimes they lied to us.
Sometimes they told us the truth.
Sometimes we hope it's the latter.
Maybe one day.
Maybe one day.
I'll know.
I'll just know.

Numbers Falling

Sydney Garcia

Ten dreams falling apart.
Nine dreams coming together.
Eight dreams given up.
Seven minds stressing more and more.
Six more weeks left.
Five new friends.
Four new companions.
Three mistakes made each day.
Two guardians.
One person with their own dream.

Ten

Angel Perez

Ten students
Ten hard workers
Ten dedicated students
Ten friendly students
Ten smart students
Ten good mathematicians
Ten science nerds
Ten good writers
Ten calm students
Ten amazing students

Seven Children

Hailee Gudrunardottir

Seven children.
Each one in here has some desire to write
They want to tell stories,
And enchant people with their words.

They work endlessly
So they can get to the top.
They get fatigued and start to wonder
When will all of this stop?

As their last days in this classroom come,
They will walk out as writers.
People who've researched and found meaning in text,
And learned from the teacher who taught it all.

Summer has arrived, and each student will begin to relax,
Thinking back to the beginning of the year,
When they were new and
They didn't know what'll hit them.

Many Students

Teandra Johnson

Many students.
Many learners.
Many daughters.
Many sons.
Many opportunities.
Many chances.
Many inspirations.
Many artists.
Many inventors.
Many hours.
Many todays.

It was a cold, dark night. Mr white were playing chess with his son Herbert as Mrs. White stands by the fire. Sergeant Morris arrives and tells them stories from when he was a soldier.

Morris then gets to a story about a paw he discovered in India. Apparently, it was cursed by an old fakir and can grant three wishes. Mr white wants the paw but Morris refuses and throws it into the fire.

Mr. White rescues the paw from the fire. White makes the first wish and he wishes for 200 hundred pounds. The paw moves and makes a crashing noise. The next day there's knock at the door.

"Who's there?" Mr. White asks while running downstairs. Mr. White proceeds to open the door only to be greeted by a man in a suit. "May I, sir?" the man asks. Mr. White lets him in. "Do you need something?" Mr. White asks. "Sir, sorry to inform you but your son Herbert has passed. Mrs. White rushes downstairs crying. "Here is your compensation of 200 pounds."

"There has to be some sort of mistake right?" Mrs. White asks while crying aloud. "I'm sorry ma'am, I'm afraid it's not. Mr. White takes the check and thanks the man while walking him out.

"Go get the paw and wish him alive!" Mrs. White screams "No the paw-" "WISH HIM ALIVE!" Mrs. White interrupts. Mr. White searches for the paw and brings it back to her.

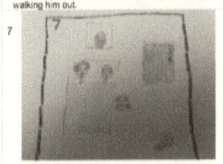

Mr. White made the wish and they went upstairs to rest. Suddenly, there was a loud knocking the door.

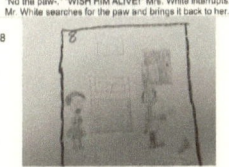

"That has to be herbert!" Mrs. White shouted as she jumped up. "Don't open it." Mr. White said while getting a flashlight. "It's your son we have to let him in!" Mrs. White yelled.

Mrs. White rushed downstairs while Mr. White tried to stop her. Mr. White is yelling from the stairs to stop her.

Mrs. White realizes she can't get to the door and needs a chair. Mr. White rushes upstairs to find the paw.

Mr. White grabbed the paw and wished. Suddenly, the knocking stopped.

When Mrs. White finally opens the door, no one is out there...

Aniyah Toomer

Bennet Cornel

2

Bennet Cornel

Bennet Cornel

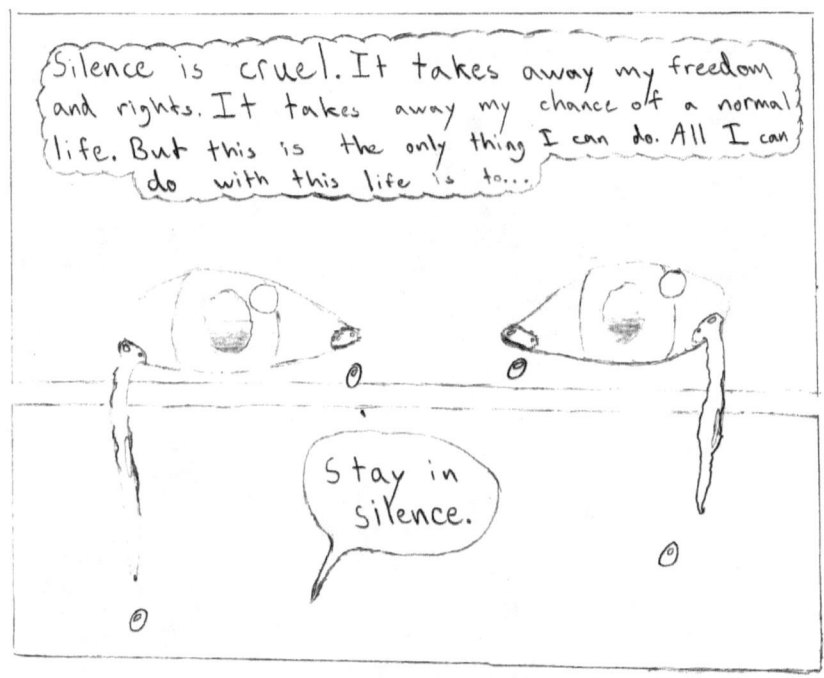

Bennet Cornel

Lilliana Baker

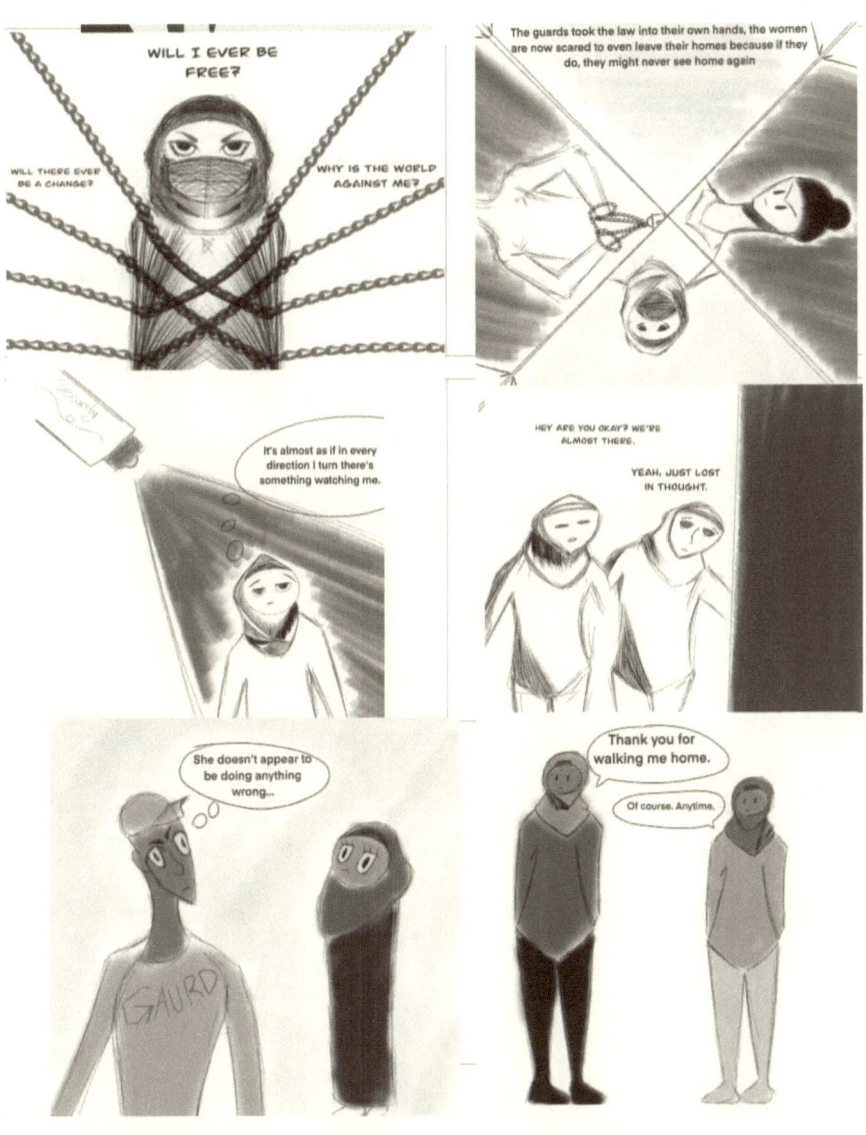

Lilliana Baker

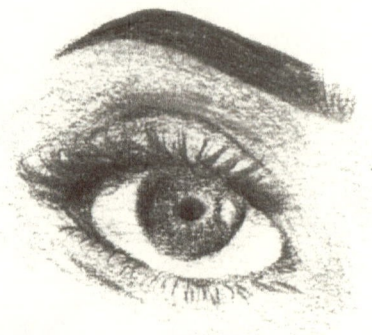
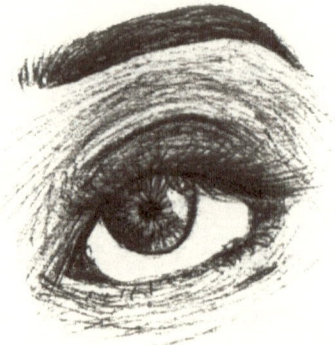

Addis Coronel

Epilogue

This year was a different kind of school year. No, no, wait, that's way too easy. Different? That barely begins to describe what we just went through. From mask mandates to mask mandates becoming optional for students with a parent waiver, schedules changing by the quarter, Zoom hacks, in-person kids huddled into the library or the computer lab ad then released to their classrooms three months in, and everything else that managed to come down, it is no wonder that this was the most stressful school year most of us have encountered. Kids vanishing into the ether of the internet only to rise again, appearing in class, or starting the year in person and finishing little more than a postage-stamp-sized face on a laptop screen was the norm. There was a lot of shuffling.

No one could say with confidence how the 2020-2021 school year would go. I mean, last year, it just ended, right in the middle of everything, weeks before a scheduled Spring Break. This year, every one of us, students and teachers alike, was flexed and twisted by the uncertainty, the bile that spewed from television screens of every ilk, division sewn at every turn. It seemed like every assurance given was haunted by the threat of doom and ruin, as students came and went, appeared and vanished into exposure quarantine, testing and retesting for Covid-19 always looming. I was tested three times and tested negative each time. Finally, when the vaccine seemed to be just out of reach for so long, with teachers pushed to the back of the line over and over again, an opportunity for vaccinations came, thanks to Mr. Perlmutter, our principal. Most of us jumped at the chance to get one, an important measure of hope restored to a bleak, challenging, and beastly year.

Don't get me wrong. Many great things came out of this experience. Canvas came along and reinvented how we teach classes, give artifacts, grade, and distribute resources. Never mind that it doubled and tripled planning time. Once we got the hang of it, it was good. I learned how to conduct a Zoom session with students that was difficult to hack, inconvenienced only a little bit by additional steps to complicate the process for those who enjoy such disruptive activities.

Students handled all of this with their usual aplomb, of course. And for the first time, Zuckerbook became an online course.

It is my sincere hope that I never again have to run this class through a Zoom feed. Our first semester had the fewest students in class ever, not one of them in my classroom. We accomplished precisely nothing. Pages and pages of content were created but left untouched for the second semester when I lost all but two of my students and had fourteen more join the fray. New ways to assign and account for work were tried, failed, tried again, succeeded in small meager ways, and continue to evolve.

And, above all, plans for a reworked Creative Writing class with Zuckerbook as its goal are now underway. Having learned the hard way and being a glutton for punishment, I have begun writing lesson plans for next year where each student will learn every facet of small-batch publishing, each step, our "corporate" identity, all of it. There will be no downtime. When the kids get "jobs" on the team, it will not be on a whim.

Having lost every on-campus fundraising opportunity due to the pandemic, we had to rely on donations and book sales to fund the printing of Zuckerbook Volume 13. Several colleagues stepped up to the plate, including Erin Presto, Steph Daniels, and Carie Tyndall. And others, like Jason Waite, Kelie James King, Rhea Farmer, Lena Viera, Eileen and Ken Babbs, Shoshana Driver, and last but never least, Clark Hilden, made it possible to finish one volume that spans the entire year. Our dedications are focused on these fine people and with good reason. Without them, you would not be reading these pages right now. And with Jacob Perlmutter leaving us for a school in need of his talent and passion, we set sail into uncharted waters, a journey across the unknown.

The writing this year, influenced heavily by the pandemic and the culture of division and anger that America has become, is darker than usual. Good! Get that out of you, I say! If you need to talk about racial unrest, then, by all means, do it. If the pandemic is causing no end of woe, release it to the written page and breathe a sigh of relief.

The students tried new things, such as focused haiku, poetry inspired by "Piecing Me Together" by Renee Watson, and poetry with specific themes, some of which worked out and some of which did not. Such is the way of the written word, you see, and they see that now, too.

I am grateful for my staff this year. All of them gave it the old college try, finding things to do and ways to finish tasks, understanding (I hope) that my being in a classroom and having many online made that difficult at best, if not impossible. But for each of our failures this year, a new approach was born that will come to fruition next year when an average (?) school year will begin this coming August. Students will be in classrooms instead of on-screen, sitting at desks that do not resemble a sea of bank-teller booths or aquariums, and we will be able to engage our learning without having to wear what feels a lot like diapers on our faces. The students came up with the idea of making this volume of Zuckerbook different - a black cover instead of our usual white, for the mourning we all feel in the wake of the death of a typical school year. They contributed the themes and chapters, the writing (but for a few strays I gleaned from the perimeter), and I believe this is among our best volumes as a result. Even our cover, still a piece by a student, was contributed by a student who came and went long ago and helped to work on the first Zuckerbook.

We as a community look back on the last ten months and sigh, wondering how we ever made it this far. How did we persevere through the constant threat of illness, the challenges of being so close and so far away at the same time? We struggled, that's for sure. Every one of us faced these difficulties, and but for a few who disappeared, made it out on the other side, more or less unscathed, ready for another year of uncertainty and stress.

Or maybe that will not be the case at all. Not one of us can know for sure which way the wind will blow come August. All I know is this: the students will come back after a painfully short Summer break, ready for a change, and we, their teachers, will be waiting for them, minds and arms open, ready to hit the ground running and keep a weather eye on the horizon.

I hope you enjoyed this volume of Zuckerbook and look forward to many more. There is a decent supply of our past volumes available on our Square Store (free shipping in the continental United States!), so give it a gander and drop us a line if you have any interest: https://zuckerbook.square.site/

Thank you yet again for your support.

With gratitude, a tip of the hat, and a big ole' smile,

Erik J. Hilden
23 May 2021